MURDER IS PARALYZING

PAULA BERNSTEIN

M&Z PRESS

This book is dedicated to Elias Meyer Bernstein
The newest and most adorable member of my family

PROLOGUE

The young blonde woman paused to take a breath as she exited the office building on Wilshire Boulevard. Traffic was still heavy even though it was almost eight p.m., and a cool breeze had followed the setting sun. She shivered, pulling her lightweight sweater more tightly around her very pregnant body. One hand touched the crucifix she wore as her only jewelry.

Was she doing the right thing? The attorney seemed to think she was, but maybe this was a huge mistake. She moved here to make a new start, to forget the nightmare, and to be anonymous. She had never told her story to anyone except her trusted priest in the privacy of the confessional.

Everything changed last week when she saw the man on television and realized how high the stakes were. She was the only one who could stop him unless he got to her first. *What would God want her to do?*

The traffic light changed. She crossed Wilshire and walked up the side street to where she'd parked her used car. As she stepped off the curb she heard an engine roaring toward her, impossibly fast and terrifyingly loud. She felt a sudden excruciating blow, a sensation of falling, and then nothing.

CHAPTER ONE

Friday October 21, 2016

D R. HANNAH KLINE OPENED HER EYES IN THE pitch dark, her heart pounding and the taste of acid reflux in her mouth. What a hideous dream! She dreamt she'd found a patient's dead body in a hospital bed and as she was bending over to check the patient's pulse, her cell phone jerked her awake.

"It's Dr. Kline. What's going on?"

"Sorry to disturb you, Doctor. We have a hit-and-run victim. She's unconscious and very pregnant. Can you come and evaluate her?"

"I'll be there in a few minutes."

Hannah flipped a switch and squinted against the bright fluorescent light in the tiny, windowless on-call room at Memorial Hospital. She couldn't have been asleep for more than half an hour. Thank goodness she only had to take Emergency Room call once every six months. She was feeling too old for this.

She spent two minutes emptying her bladder, splashed

some cold water on her face, pulled her long red hair into a ponytail, and put on a white coat over her wrinkled scrubs. Then she walked through the double doors.

The emergency room was relatively empty, compared to how packed it had been earlier in the evening. Hannah had already taken care of several miscarriages and operated on a ruptured tubal pregnancy. She had hoped she was finished for the night.

She saw a crowd around a bed in one of the trauma rooms and headed in that direction. The patient was a visibly pregnant young woman. Her skin was pale and pasty, her face swollen and bruised, her light blonde hair soaked in blood. She wore a gold cross on a delicate chain around her neck.

"Hi, Hannah." Dr. Jai Patel, the good-looking Indian ER doc, had just drawn multiple tubes of blood and was handing them to one of the nurses.

Hannah gave him a wave and a smile. "What's the story?"

Patel shrugged. "A couple returning home from a dinner out found her lying in the street and called 911. The EMTs had no idea how long she'd been there, but from the trauma they were sure she'd been hit by a car."

"Do we know who she is?"

"No purse, no wallet, no phone, no ID. We'll have to wait until she regains consciousness to get her contact information and notify her family."

Hannah turned to the OB resident on call. "What's the status of the pregnancy?"

"I got a heartbeat. I was just about to do an ultrasound for dating and to make sure the placenta wasn't bleeding."

"We can look together. What about her vitals? Any sign of a brain bleed?"

"Vitals are stable," Patel said. "We're evaluating her neurological status right now. Have you met Dr. Roger Geller? He's a neurosurgeon."

Geller was a tall, completely bald man with a bushy gray mustache, who was shining a light into the woman's pupils.

"I've heard your name, but we haven't met," Hannah said. "I'm Hannah Kline, the OB attending. What's her neuro status?"

"She's unconscious. I'm going to need a CT to evaluate her brain for a bleed and to check for fractures."

Hannah watched as the resident squeezed ultrasound gel onto the woman's abdomen and began the scan. "The baby is vertex. His head diameter is consistent with 38 weeks, there's plenty of amniotic fluid, and he's active."

"Those are all good signs. I don't see any evidence of a placental bleed," Hannah said.

"I want to take her to CT now," Geller said.

The woman moaned and her eyelids fluttered.

"Don't be afraid," Patel said. "You've had an accident and you're in the hospital. We're going to take good care of you."

She opened her eyes. They were deep blue and moved frantically around the room.

"I can't move my hands," she said.

Dr Geller reached for a needle and took her hand in his, placing two fingers on her palm.

"Squeeze my hand," he said.

There was no movement.

He took the needle and began working his way up her arm. "Tell me when you feel something sharp."

"I can't feel anything," she said. As the needle reached her shoulder she winced. "I felt that."

"Let's check your feet. Can you wiggle your toes?"

She couldn't, and had no response as he moved the needle up her leg.

"You seem to have an injury to your spine," Dr. Geller said. "We're going to send you for a scan. Once I can see the damage, we'll take you to surgery to fix it."

A look of panic crossed the woman's face.

Hannah leaned over and touched her shoulder. "I'm Dr. Kline. I want you to know your baby is fine. He wasn't injured in the accident."

"What baby? I don't have a baby!"

"Not yet," Hannah said, "but it looks as if you're due to deliver in about two weeks."

"I'm pregnant!" She couldn't have looked more astonished.

"Can you tell me your name," Geller asked.

"It's Nicole, Nicole Adler."

"Nicole, can we call someone for you, your husband or parents?"

"I don't think I have a husband or parents. I can't think of anyone."

Two orderlies with a gurney and a transfer board entered the room.

"Nicole, let's get a scan and see what we need to do to help you. Then we can figure everything else out," Hannah said. "Would you like me to come with you to radiology?"

"Please," Nicole whispered. "I've never been so scared."

CHAPTER TWO

Friday, October 21, 2016

HANNAH WALKED ALONGSIDE THE GURNEY SO THAT Nicole could see her. Dr. Geller followed behind. The orderlies took the patient into the CT room and helped the X-ray tech transfer her to the table. Hannah and Geller waited in the control room, where they could see the images as they came up on the computer.

"Do you think she's going to be permanently paralyzed?" Hannah asked.

"Depends on how severe the injury is. I'll have a better idea in a few minutes."

The tech came out of the CT scan room and activated the scan. Slices of the brain began to appear.

"Damn it. She's got a bleed in the left temporal region. I'm going to have to evacuate the blood. That's the priority."

"Could that account for why she didn't seem to remember she was pregnant?" Hannah asked.

"Probably. Once the brain swelling goes down we'll see how far back her memories go. Brain injuries like this can cause retrograde amnesia, although some memories will return with time."

"Poor woman. No wonder she looked terrified."

The cervical spine images began to load.

"She's got a fracture at the level of the fifth cervical vertebrae," Geller said. "Can you see where the bone is shattered? It looks like there's a hematoma in the space surrounding the spinal cord. She's going to have major deficits."

"I feel so sorry for her," Hannah said. "What about the pregnancy? Is it going to make your surgery more difficult or dangerous?"

"You can deliver her by caesarian section while I do the brain surgery. Then we turn her over and address the spinal compression. That way, the baby won't be compromised. Call your people and have them bring the C-Section equipment to the neurosurgery floor."

Hannah gritted her teeth. She didn't appreciate being talked to as if she were a medical student.

"I've already told my resident to notify Labor and Delivery. I'm just waiting for you to tell us which OR and what time."

"Good. My team will set up. We'll take her directly to pre-op from here. The labs should be back by now, and the scan's about done."

"That means we need to go in there and do the hard part," Hannah said. "It's a lot of bad news to absorb at once."

"When you're a neurosurgeon, the news is rarely good," Geller said. "At least you get to tell her she has a healthy baby."

"I can't imagine how she's going to take care of him," Hannah said.

～

Nicole lay on a gurney in pre-op, her head and neck firmly stabilized in a brace. She could see the huge bulge of her belly under the flimsy white blanket. It was unbelievable that she was pregnant. She couldn't remember a boyfriend, or a husband, or any doctor visits.

Maybe this whole thing is a bad dream. When I wake up, I'll be thin, and able to move and scratch the itch on my nose.

"Nicole, Dr. Geller and I need you to consent for your surgeries," Dr. Kline said. "These two people are from our legal department. They're here to witness your consent since you can't sign your name."

Nicole looked up at the crowd that had materialized by her bed. Dr. Kline was holding a clipboard with papers. She had a pretty face with green eyes. Wisps of red hair peeked out from her paper surgical cap. Something about the warmth in her expression made Nicole trust her.

"Would you like to read the consent? I can hold it and turn the pages for you, or we can read it aloud."

"Read it please," Nicole said. "I suppose a normal delivery is out of the question?"

"Absolutely. Not under these circumstances. We need to take care of the blood clot on your brain and your cervical spine fracture as quickly as possible," Dr. Geller said.

"Just asking."

Dr. Geller read the consent for a craniotomy with evacuation of the blood clot and a cervical laminectomy, with decompression of the spine and insertion of rods. He explained the surgery in detail. "Any questions, Ms. Adler?"

"Will I be able to move once the surgery is over?"

"We won't know until the swelling goes down. We'll be giving you steroids to help with that and pain medication."

"I consent," Nicole said. She had no choice. "Will my

memory come back? I'd like to know who fathered this baby."

"We're going to work on finding out everything we can about you," Dr. Kline said. "Once we've tracked down your family and friends, you'll have more information to help jog your memory."

"People with brain injuries and some degree of amnesia usually regain memory over time," Dr. Geller added.

"I hope so. Is someone going to find out whose car hit me and caused all of this?"

"You bet," Dr. Kline said. "I happen to know a police detective who could do just that.

CHAPTER THREE

Saturday, October 22, 2016

HANNAH MADE AN INCISION INTO NICOLE'S abdomen, with her resident assisting. As she worked her way through the tissue layers she heard Geller giving instructions to the anesthesiologist. It was odd, doing a Caesarian under general anesthesia. Usually, the mother was awake with an epidural and got to see her baby within a minute of delivery. Of course, this was out of the question with a spinal cord injury.

As Hannah reached the uterus she heard the sound of Geller drilling holes into Nicole's skull. Of all the surgeries she could think of, craniotomy was number one on her list of procedures she hoped never to have. A shiver ran up her back as she reached her hand in and followed the curve of the baby's head, deep into the pelvis and delivered it, followed immediately by the shoulders and remainder of the body.

The baby gave a loud cry as Hannah cleared the mucus from his nose and mouth with a bulb syringe.

"Looks like a healthy boy," she commented, as she handed him to a pediatrician. At the same moment, she saw Geller hand a piece of skull to a nurse, and Hannah watched as clots were suctioned from the space between the brain and the dura mater membrane.

"Is she bleeding actively?" she asked.

"I'm irrigating now. I don't think so. Everything okay at your end?"

"I just have to remove the placenta and close."

"Vitals holding steady," the anesthesiologist said.

Hannah returned her attention to her patient and waited for the uterus to contract, pulling gently on the umbilical cord to extract the placenta. She examined it for evidence of injury but found nothing obvious. It was fortunate that the car hadn't hit directly on her belly. If it had, the placenta would probably have detached, and both mother and child would have bled to death before she was found.

She let the resident close, and when they were done, went to post-op to dictate her operative report. Then she examined the earliest computer notes on Nicole's admission. To her relief, the EMT who brought her in had documented the contact information of the couple who found her, the location, and included his phone number and email. Daniel would need all of this to get started.

She glanced at her watch. It was just after 4:00 a.m.. No point in calling him now. He was home with Zoe and they would still be asleep. Her shift would be ending at 7:00 a.m. She would call him then.

She asked the charge nurse to notify her when Nicole was brought into post-op and retreated to the on-call room to get some rest. She set her phone alarm for 6:30 a.m. and collapsed onto the hard, single bed. Within moments, she was asleep.

Daniel woke slowly, rolling over and feeling the cold bed linen. He never slept quite as well when Hannah was on call. Even though she and Daniel did their best to arrange their schedules so that someone was always home for Zoe, and to manage some weekends when both of them were off, this weekend was a double whammy for her. She was on ER call on Friday night and on call for her practice on Saturday and Sunday.

As he opened his eyes, his cell phone rang.

He answered it. "Hi, love, did you get any sleep?"

"Hardly any. I need a favor. The EMTs brought in a hit-and-run victim last night. She was pregnant and had both a brain and spinal cord injury. Could you look into it? I'll text you the details."

"Do you know if anyone made a police report?"

"I don't."

"I'll check and see what I can find. When will you be home?"

"My shift's over, but I want to go see her in the ICU, and I have a few other patients to make rounds on. I should be home no later than 8:00, but don't count on me to be conscious."

"No worries. I'll make you breakfast and tuck you in without demanding any scintillating conversation. And Zoe has a play date at Andrea's today. But, sweetheart, I may not be able to investigate this hit-and-run. It's not a homicide."

"It's worse than a homicide. If my patient can't move and can't remember her past, or any friends or family, her life is over. She's as good as dead."

CHAPTER FOUR

Saturday, October 22, 2016

NICOLE OPENED HER EYES SLOWLY, TRYING TO adjust to the bright light. She was in a small room with a glass wall looking toward a central station. She felt pain in the back of her neck and shoulders but the rest of her body was numb.

Dr. Kline came through the door smiling. She wore scrubs, and a halo of curly red hair surrounded her face.

"Good morning. I see you're awake. Are you in any pain?"

"Just my neck and head. How did the surgery go? Am I going to be able to move?"

"The neurosurgeon says it's too early to tell. He stabilized your spine and took care of the blood clot in your brain, but we'll have to wait for all the swelling and inflammation to resolve to see where you are. I know it's hard to have patience, but you're in the ICU and getting the best possible care."

"I can see my big belly is gone. Did you deliver the baby? Was it...healthy?"

Dr. Kline reached into her breast pocket and pulled out a Polaroid photo. "I did. You had a Cesarean section and a baby boy. I went to the nursery this morning to check on him and took a picture for you."

She walked over to the side of the bed and held it so Nicole could see. The baby was in a plastic cradle, wrapped in a blanket. His face was round and rosy, his hair dark, and his wide eyes a deep blue. He looked pretty cute, but she couldn't see herself in his features.

"I can have the nurse bring him to you later this morning." Dr. Kline said. She taped the photo to the bed railing where Nicole could see it.

"I can't move. I can't nurse him. I don't have anyone to help me. What am I going to do with a baby?"

Dr Kline came closer and put a hand on Nicole's shoulder. "We'll help you nurse, Nicole, and some of your memories should come back. You might find that you have people who want to be here for you. Can you recall anything about the accident?"

"Nothing. Where was I found?"

"You were on a residential street, not far from Wilshire and La Cienega."

"Wilshire? Wait. There's no Wilshire in Manhattan."

"Nicole, you're in Los Angeles. Do you remember coming here?"

Her mind was blank. The most recent memory she could access was being in her studio apartment in Chelsea. She was sure she lived alone. What was she doing in LA?

"I'm from New York. I don't remember coming here or living here."

"Can you remember your New York address or occupation?"

"I'm an actress and a model. I do more modeling than acting. It's hard to get a job in the theater. I live on West 17th Street just off 10th Avenue."

"That helps a great deal. Are you on social media?"

"Of course. Mostly Instagram."

"I'm going to go online and see what I can find out about you. Hopefully, when I come in to see you again, I'll have information that will help you remember. In the meantime, I want to listen to your lungs and check your incision."

While the doctor was listening to her breathe, Nicole tried to recall everything she could about her family. She was sure she was an only child, and her parents...they were gone. Her grandmother lived in New Jersey, but Gram was in a nursing home in the last stages of dementia.

What about friends? A parade of faces crossed her mind, but none of them registered as someone who would or could fly across the country to help a paralyzed person care for herself and an infant. Why couldn't she remember who the father was?

Dr Kline looked up. "Is there anything you'd like me to order for you before I leave? Pain medicine? Breakfast?"

"Something for pain would be nice," Nicole said. "And I would like to see the baby. Please let me know as soon as you find out anything about me."

"I will."

Nicole watched as the doctor left the room, had a word with the nurse, and sat down at a computer terminal. A few moments later, the nurse came in with a syringe and inserted it into the IV port.

Pain gradually subsided, and Nicole slipped into a healing sleep.

CHAPTER FIVE

Saturday October 22nd, 2016

IT WAS 8:30 A.M. BEFORE HANNAH MADE IT HOME after rounds. Daniel and Zoe were in the kitchen.

"Hi, Mommy. We waited for you for breakfast. We're making chocolate chip pancakes. Are you hungry?"

"Starved," Hannah said, depositing a kiss on Zoe's forehead.

"You look tired," Daniel said. "All-nighter?"

"Pretty much. I'm going to need a nap after breakfast."

"You should have been an eye doctor, Mommy. No one has a glasses emergency at night."

"Good point." Hannah sat down at the kitchen table and poured herself a mug of coffee, as she watched Daniel spoon pancake batter onto the griddle. She was more exhausted than hungry, but she appreciated the nurturing. She dug in when Zoe brought her a plate and a jug of warm maple syrup.

When they finished eating, Daniel cleared the table and turned to Zoe.

"Why don't you go upstairs and get dressed? I'll drive you to your play date, and we'll let your mother get some sleep."

Zoe left the room, and Daniel turned to Hannah. "Sounds like it was a particularly awful night."

"It was heartbreaking, Daniel. The poor woman is likely to be a quadriplegic. She can't remember anything in the immediate past, including the father of her baby. She didn't even remember that she's in Los Angeles. But I told her I knew a brilliant police detective and would do my best to help her."

"Were you able to learn anything else about her since we spoke?"

Hannah nodded and briefed him.

"I'm on it. I'll find out about the accident, and run her name through all my databases. I'll check out her Instagram. Print some photos that might trigger memories for her."

"That would be great, sweetheart. I'd love to find family who could help her."

After dropping Zoe off, Daniel headed to his desk at the station to check the police databases. The name and address information led to a driver's license, photo, birth certificate, and death certificates for Nicole Adler's parents. A careful check revealed no siblings and no marriage license.

Nicole had a college degree from Rutgers and had lived in New York City since graduating in 2011. There was no record of any arrest or criminal behavior. Google found her photo on the roster of New York Star Models and in several fashion catalogs. Daniel also found her mentioned in reviews of two small off-Broadway plays in 2013.

His next step should be Instagram, but Daniel hesitated. Not only did he consider social media a waste of time, it raised significant security concerns, which is why he avoided being on any of the platforms. He'd never post anything personal about himself or his family online, where it could be available to the criminals he jailed and their associates. He believed his private life should be private.

Of course, he had access to all the sites via law enforcement but, like Hannah, he was a social media Luddite. It was easier to rely on his younger colleagues to navigate social media and a better use of his energy to find out the status of the hit-and-run. He picked up his phone and rang dispatch.

"It's Detective Ross. There was a hit-and-run last night. Can you tell me who's in charge of the investigation?"

"It's Leila Abebe, the new detective transfer from Hollenbeck. Have you met her?

"Not yet. Is she in, by any chance?"

"Yeah. Check the pit. She arrived earlier than you did."

Daniel got up and searched the room. He spotted a woman he didn't know in a cubicle at the other end. "Hi, are you Detective Abebe?"

She looked up. Daniel saw a face with high cheekbones, deep brown skin, and closely cut curly hair.

"Can I help you?"

Daniel smiled and held out his hand. "Detective Daniel Ross, homicide. Welcome to the Westside. Can I ask you a few questions about the hit and run you caught last night?"

"Sure. Is it related to a case you're working on?"

Daniel took a seat, shaking his head. "Not exactly. My

wife Hannah is an ob-gyn at Memorial. She took care of the victim."

"I don't know how much I can tell you. I haven't been able to speak to the victim. The hospital said she was in surgery when I called late last night. I'll try again tomorrow."

"When you speak to her, you'll discover that she has a serious brain injury and amnesia. She was able to tell Hannah her name and New York address but was surprised to learn she was in Los Angeles and pregnant. She may not be able to tell you anything helpful about the accident, because she doesn't remember."

"How badly was she injured?" Abebe asked.

"Very. She's likely to be quadriplegic in addition to having a traumatic brain injury. Hannah had to deliver her baby by c-section, so that the neurosurgeon could operate."

"That's awful."

"Hannah asked me to do a database search and see if I could find any family or photos that might jog her memory."

"Did you?"

Daniel summarized his findings. "I know she has a presence on Instagram. She's a model and actress. I haven't looked through her account yet because I'm not very familiar with Instagram. Maybe we could look together."

Abebe grinned. "Sure. I just finished reviewing the security tapes my guys got from the homeowners on the street where she was hit. I can show you what I found."

"Great."

"When it comes to Instagram, it's easier to check it on a phone. "That specific platform was built for mobile devices. We can look through it now. If we find anything useful, I'll send it to my email and print it for you. Then I'll show you the tapes."

Daniel pulled his chair around so he could see her screen. By the time he got home, he should have something to share with Hannah.

CHAPTER SIX

Saturday October 22nd, 2016

NICOLE SPENT THE MORNING DRIFTING IN AND OUT of a morphine-induced haze. Her neck incision hurt and she had a throbbing headache. Her body felt like a dead weight. Periodically she would try to wiggle her toes or make a fist, but her brain seemed disconnected from her limbs.

The neurosurgeon, Dr. Geller, appeared in Nicole's room just before noon, trailed by a group of white-coated residents and medical students.

"Good morning, Ms. Adler." He turned to the nearest young doctor. "Give us a summary, please."

Glancing at an iPad, the resident cleared his throat. "Ms. Adler was admitted to the ER last night, the victim of a hit and run. She was approximately 38 weeks pregnant and sustained a skull fracture and subdural hematoma in the temporal region, as well as a fracture of the C5 vertebra. She underwent an emergency Cesarean section, a craniotomy with evacuation of the hematoma, and a C4-C6 spinal fusion. She has significant retrograde amnesia and the neurological exam is currently consistent with quadriplegia."

Geller nodded and turned to her. "Let's examine you and see how you are doing today. Are you in pain?"

"Not much. The nurses have been giving me medication for my neck and headache. I can't feel anything else."

Geller took out a small flashlight, examined her pupils, and checked her neck incision. He then repeated his previous examination of her reflexes and tested her sensation with a needle, nodding to himself as he proceeded.

"Is this going to get any better?" Nicole asked.

"We won't know for several days. In the meantime, I'll have you evaluated by our rehabilitation team. They will start you on some range of motion exercises. Our occupational therapist will assess your needs and see how we can help."

"I'm an actress and a model. If this doesn't get better, I'll need a new occupation." Tears began to form. She blinked hard to prevent them from pouring over her cheeks. Crying in front of all these people wasn't an option.

"I'll see you tomorrow," Geller said, leaving the room with his entourage trailing behind him.

Nicole's ICU nurse entered, carrying a tray. "It's lunchtime. Are you hungry?"

"A little."

"Tuna salad, vanilla yogurt, and some fresh fruit."

"Let's start with the yogurt," Nicole said.

The nurse draped a napkin over her chest, picked up a spoon, and began to feed her. It was humiliating.

"Any trouble swallowing?"

"No." After finishing the yogurt, she ate the fruit,

chewing thoroughly and washing down each mouthful with sips of water, administered through a straw.

"Would you like to see your baby this afternoon? I can bring him up."

"I won't be able to hold him," Nicole said.

"I'll help. Don't worry. We're all here to do whatever you need."

The nurse reached for some tissues. She blotted Nicole's cheeks and helped her blow her nose.

Half an hour later, the nurse wheeled a bassinet into the room. She brought Nicole's hospital bed to a sitting position and arranged her arms on a pillow. The nurse held the baby so that Nicole could see her son. His little face was round, pink and flawless. Perfect lips made a sucking motion and a tiny hand emerged from his pale blue blanket. He was enchanting.

The nurse lifted him and placed him on Nicole's chest, his head in the crook of her neck. Nicole smelled the intoxicating scent of baby powder. He had the softest skin she'd ever felt. A wave of love for this tiny, helpless being arose in her chest and moved to her lips. Shrugging her shoulder to bring him closer, she bent and kissed his forehead.

"Would you like to nurse him?"

"I'll try."

The nurse closed the blinds for privacy and loosened Nicole's hospital gown to reveal her breasts. Placing the baby on a pillow in Nicole's lap, she adjusted his head so that he could reach a nipple. He latched on immediately and began to suck.

"He's got the hang of it."

"Can I do this?" Nicole watched as her son fed.

"I think you can. I'm going to order you some nursing hospital gowns. Have you thought about a name?"

"I still can't remember anything about getting pregnant or being pregnant. Dr. Kline said she would research social media and see what she could find out about me. Maybe that will help me remember." She looked at the baby and thought about names. "Maybe I'll name him after my Dad, Gerald. What do you think of Jeremy?"

"It's a beautiful name."

Hannah napped until mid-afternoon, took a hot shower, and put on clean clothes. Then she fixed herself a cup of chai latte and retrieved her non-emergency phone messages. Luckily, no patient from their practice had gone into labor. She didn't have the energy for another all-night marathon.

The door opened and Daniel came into the kitchen. She got up and hugged him."

"Feeling rested?"

"Much better. I wonder how long it will take before I'm too old for all this."

"A few more decades, I suspect. If you didn't love it, you wouldn't do it."

"Says the man who examines dead bodies in the middle of the night."

Daniel laughed. "I don't love the dead bodies, but I do like the challenge of solving cases and getting some justice for the victim's family."

"Speaking of victims, any information?"

Daniel nodded. His face became serious. "I got some

useful information online about your patient, but the most important news came from the detective who caught the hit-and-run. It was in a residential area and several homes had security cameras that covered the street. When your patient crossed, the van that hit her accelerated from a dead stop. It wasn't an accident. It was attempted murder."

CHAPTER SEVEN

Sunday, October 23, 2016

HANNAH BEGAN HER SUNDAY MORNING ROUNDS AT 7:30 a.m. so that the day shift of nurses would be available for her orders. She saved the surgical ICU for last.

Nicole was sitting up, a tray table in front of her, being fed by a clinical nurse partner. She stopped eating when she spotted Hannah.

"Go ahead and finish your breakfast," Hannah said. "I'll review your chart. We can talk when you're done eating."

"There's only so much hospital oatmeal a girl can eat," Nicole said. "Please, come in."

The aide removed the tray and left the room. Hannah closed the door behind her.

"I'm glad to see you alert. How was yesterday?"

"Terrifying. I doubt I'll ever be able to move again and I still can't remember anything about Los Angeles or the accident. On the plus side, I nursed the baby."

"I'm impressed," Hannah said. "Nursing can be a challenge under the best of circumstances."

"I should probably stop," Nicole said. "If I don't, I'm going to fall in love with him and I know I can't care for him. I've been thinking about my options, but the only viable one is adoption."

Hannah sat down on the chair nearest the bed. "You don't have to make that decision right now. Give us time to track down the father and any extended family you have, and give yourself time for some of your memories to return. It's only post-op day one. A great deal can change in a few days."

"Did you find out anything?"

Hannah nodded. "Let me check your incision and listen to your lungs. Then I can show you what we found on the internet."

After assuring herself that her patient's surgical status was stable, Hannah opened her tote bag and extracted a pile of papers.

"We verified your identity with a birth certificate, driver's license and college degree. We also found a number of photos in your Instagram account. You posted a lot in January and then you stopped. I printed everything out. Do you recognize any of the names or faces on these pictures or remember anything about this party?"

Hannah held up the photos, one at a time. They documented an upscale event. Nicole looked stunning in a strapless emerald green dress and dangling gold earrings. She was with other beautifully dressed and made-up young women and men in tuxedos. They were all holding glasses of champagne. The women were young. The men were older.

"The location for these photos is New York City, on West 56th Street and 5th Avenue. There are names on the photos. Do you recognize anyone?"

Nicole shook her head. "None of the names are familiar, but I think I know these two women. I feel as if I like them, but I don't remember anything specific."

Hannah glanced at the names. Brittany Miller was a tall brunette with a wide smile and a curvaceous figure. Emily Harris was petite and blonde with a short, geometric haircut.

"Do you recognize any of the men in the photos? Could one of them be a date or a boyfriend?"

"They all look twenty years older than anyone I would date. I'm wondering if this is some kind of photo shoot. It doesn't look like any party I'd be invited to. I'm sure I couldn't afford that designer dress and I'd rather drink beer than champagne."

Hannah continued showing the photos, giving Nicole time to examine each one.

Nicole caught her breath. "This guy. I hate him and I'm frightened of him, but I don't know why."

"Let me see."

The photo showed Nicole standing near a baby grand piano. A man in the background was staring at her. He was tall and overweight with a tuxedo jacket that pulled across his abdomen. His hair was gray and balding, and he had a prominent nose and double chin. Bushy eyebrows framed penetrating dark eyes.

"Why don't I look up these two women, and see if I can get in touch? They might be friends who would know where these photos were taken and help us figure out how you wound up in Los Angeles."

"I'd appreciate any help you can provide. I'm so scared. Tell me the truth, Dr. Kline. Am I ever going to be able to move again or remember anything about my life?"

"The truth is that I don't know. We have to wait for the

swelling to subside. I can only imagine how frightened you are, but I'll do whatever I can to help you. The best thing you can do is focus on getting through your recovery, one day at a time."

Hannah arrived home to find Daniel and Zoe playing soccer in the backyard.

"Hi, Mommy." Zoe kicked the ball in Hannah's direction and Hannah attempted to pass it to Daniel. It landed in the pool.

"You have lousy aim," Daniel said with a grin.

"We didn't play soccer in Brooklyn when I was growing up. Besides, you guys know I'm a couch potato."

"Then you should help me finish my homework," Zoe announced. "You haven't been home all weekend."

"I know, sweetie. I'm sorry. Sometimes my work gets a little overwhelming, and this weekend was one of those times. Give me about half an hour and I'm all yours."

Zoe took off her sneakers and socks, pulled the ball toward the pool edge with a long-handled net, and stepped into the water to retrieve it. "Ouch, it's cold."

"Good job," Daniel said.

Zoe made a face, threw the ball onto a chair, and retreated into the house.

"Any news?" Daniel asked.

"I've got three names I need to track down," Hannah said. "Two of them may be friends of my patient and might know some more information about her. One is a man. Nicole had a bad feeling about him but didn't know why."

"You're going all out for this woman, Hannah."

"Of course, I am. She's a new mother and the victim of a murder attempt. Wouldn't you?"

"Yeah, I would. Some people just make you want to run the extra mile. Why don't you give me the names and I'll do the investigating. Zoe was a bit cranky today. I think she needs her mom."

CHAPTER EIGHT

Monday, October 24th, 2016

W HEN DANIEL ARRIVED AT THE STATION ON Monday morning, he found Leila Abebe at her desk. He grabbed a mug of coffee from the station kitchen and walked over.

"I see you're an early bird. Any progress?" Leila looked up from her computer.

"We found the van on a side street off the 10 Freeway. It had been stolen. We're checking it for fingerprints and DNA."

"My wife showed all the Instagram photos to the victim yesterday. She recognized two women and one man, but couldn't remember who they were. She just had feelings about them."

"What kind of feelings?"

"Nice ones about the women. I think they were friends, models from the same agency. I was hoping you could get contact information from the agency this morning." Daniel handed her a printout of the labeled photo of Nicole, flanked by the two women.

"What about the man?" Leila asked.

"Nicole felt frightened of him. He's not labeled, so we need to find other photos of the event on social media or do facial recognition. At least we know the date."

Leila looked at her watch. "I need to run. I'm going to Memorial this morning to see Nicole."

"Maybe she'll remember something more," Daniel said. "Listen, I have some spare time this morning. If you like, I can make a few calls and try to get hold of the two women."

"Why are you so interested in this case? It's not a homicide."

"Hannah's concerned about her patient. And something I find out might help jog her memory."

Leila bristled. "I don't want you violating confidentiality in an ongoing case and getting me into trouble. You can make the calls, tell me what you learned, and I'll decide what, if anything, you can share with your wife."

"Deal," Daniel said.

He'd initially liked this new detective. Now he wasn't so sure. Technically, he was her superior and he had seniority. She could be a little more deferential.

When he returned to his desk, his partner Brenda Jordan was staring at her computer, drinking coffee. She turned to face him, her blonde bob swinging around her face, and gave him a big smile.

Brenda had been remarkably relaxed and happy since her recent wedding to Marcy and her decision to come out to her parents and at work. The news had unearthed a few dicks among the rank and file, but her strong support from the chief had taken care of them. They might be thinking nasty thoughts but they kept their mouths shut in her presence.

"You look happy. Good weekend?"

"Great weekend. Marcy and I went out for Chinese. If it stays this quiet, I'll be all caught up on my paperwork. How about you?"

Daniel took a seat. "I wound up doing some work on a hit and run."

"Why? That's not normally our department."

"Hannah asked me to look into it. She was on ER call this weekend and a pregnant patient came in who was badly injured. Turns out the hit and run was an attempted murder. It left the victim with a brain injury, amnesia, and paralyzed from the neck down."

"Sounds heartbreaking and frustrating," Brenda said.

"It was. Hannah's trying to help. Unfortunately, nothing she does is going to make any medical difference."

"That's so sad. I'm happy to hold down the fort if you want to keep looking into it. I'll page you if we get a homicide case."

CHAPTER NINE

Monday, October 24th, 2016

DANIEL PHONED NEW YORK STAR MODELS AFTER Leila Abebe left the station. "My name is Daniel Ross. I'm calling from Los Angeles. I want to contact two of your models, Brittany Miller and Emily Harris."

"Is this regarding a photo shoot, Mr. Ross?" the receptionist said.

"No, it's regarding Nicole Adler."

"Nicole doesn't work for us any longer. She left the agency about six months ago."

"Yes, I know that. Nicole asked me to contact these two women. They're friends."

"Well, it's against our policy to give out personal contact information, Mr. Ross, but if you leave your number, I can call and give them your message.

Daniel took a breath. Nothing was easy these days. "Please ask them to call Detective Ross at the Los Angeles Police Department." He gave her his number and work email, hung up, and returned to his cases.

Nicole was being fed a breakfast of scrambled eggs and white toast when a tall, dark-skinned woman, conservatively dressed in slacks and a blue blazer appeared in her doorway.

"Miss Adler?"

"Are you the social worker?" Nicole had asked to see one today. If she ever recovered enough to get out of here, she had no idea where to go, how to live, and what to do with Jeremy. She was desperate for help.

"No, I'm Detective Abebe. Do you feel up to answering a few questions today? I'm in charge of finding the person responsible for putting you in the hospital."

"I can talk to you, but they've probably told you I can't remember the accident. Would you like to sit down?"

The detective pulled up the only chair in the room and seated herself toward the end of the bed so Nicole could make eye contact. Abebe pulled out a notebook and pen and crossed her legs.

"Do you recall what you were doing on Willaman Drive?"

"Is that where the accident was?"

The detective nodded. "Just north of Wilshire, but it wasn't an accident."

"What do you mean, it wasn't an accident? What else could it have been?"

"We have security footage showing that the driver deliberately accelerated to hit you. We're considering this attempted murder. Do you have any idea who might want to kill you?"

"Kill me? Why would anyone want to do that? I don't even know anyone in Los Angeles."

The thought that a killer was after her filled Nicole with terror. She was helpless to defend herself. Anyone could walk in here, smother her, inject poison into her IV, even stab her to death, and get away with it.

"Do you have an ex-husband or boyfriend? An angry business partner?"

"I don't have anyone. I don't remember anyone! You've terrified me. If you think someone wants me dead, then protect me."

The detective closed her notebook and stood. She was finished with her questioning. "I'm assigning an officer to guard you twenty-four-seven until we've solved this. I'm going to leave you my card. If you remember anything that could help, call me."

"Can I have my purse and my phone? My contact list might jog my memory."

Detective Abebe hesitated.

"Oh! Did you take it for evidence?"

"We couldn't find it. It wasn't at the scene. The person who hit you probably took it."

Nicole felt panic rising within her as the detective left the room. *Why couldn't she remember the man who fathered her baby? Could he want to kill both of them? Had she been having an affair? Was there a jealous wife?* None of it made sense. But there was something about Willaman Drive that sounded vaguely familiar.

A new nurse walked in to check her vitals. She was short and squat with gray hair. She reminded Nicole of someone. The image of a gray-haired woman sitting behind a desk in an elegant office flashed through her thoughts. *Who was she and did she have anything to do with the murder attempt?*

~

It was lunchtime before Daniel's cell phone finally rang with a New York number.

"Detective Ross?"

"Speaking."

"This is Brittany Miller. You wanted to speak to me about Nicole. Has something happened to her?"

"She's had an accident, Ms. Miller, and is in the hospital. The accident resulted in a head injury and temporary amnesia. Nicole recognized your face on Instagram and thought you might be a friend."

"How do I know that you're a detective? I'm not answering any questions until I get proof."

"Fair enough," Daniel said. "Write down this number. It's the main telephone line for the West Los Angeles LAPD. You can verify it by googling it on your computer or phone. Ask the desk sergeant for Detective Ross and he will transfer you."

A few minutes later his landline rang. "Detective Ross speaking."

"Okay, detective. What do you need to know?"

"Are you a friend of Nicole Adler?" Daniel asked.

"I am, or I was before she left town."

"When was that?"

"Toward the end of March. Nicole said she was going to L.A. for an audition and might stay for a while and see if she could break into film. I spoke to her once or twice after that. She was working a temporary waitressing job and doing auditions, but after a while, she ghosted me. I called and texted but she never answered."

"When she was in New York, did she have a boyfriend?"

"No one steady. She dated occasionally, but most of the men who come on to models only want to get laid and

Nicole wanted a relationship. I don't know if she had better luck in LA."

Daniel opened his desk drawer and took out the photos he had printed out.

"Can we FaceTime for a few minutes? I'll call you back from my cell phone. I have some photographs I'd like to show you."

Brittany's face appeared on Daniel's screen. Unlike the glamour photos he'd seen, she wore no makeup. Her dark hair was in a ponytail and she was wearing a *Nasty Woman* T-shirt. He held up the photo of Nicole, flanked by her two friends.

"This is the last thing she posted on Instagram. Do you recognize this party?"

"Oh yeah. That was a fundraiser at Fuchs Tower. The agency was asked to provide as many models as they had available for the event. It was old rich guys, without their wives, socializing with beautiful young women. I didn't know all the ladies. I have a hunch some of them were professionals, if you get my drift."

"I do," Daniel said. "Do you recognize the man standing behind you, holding the glass of champagne?"

Brittany's lips pursed. "Yeah. I think he had the hots for Nicole. She was looking particularly gorgeous. He came over and started a conversation with her after we took the photo."

"What did she do?

Brittany shrugged. "We were being extremely well paid to be beautiful, polite and charming to these old geezers. She talked to him."

"Do you know if they had sex?"

"We're models, not call girls. You couldn't pay any of us enough to fuck a disgusting old Fuchs supporter."

"Do you know if Nicole had much to drink that night?"

"I doubt it. Nicole was very straight. She grew up in a religious Catholic family. She rarely had more than one drink, didn't smoke or do drugs, and didn't sleep around."

"Did you see Nicole leave the party?"

"No. Emily and I shared a cab home. We both live on the Upper West Side. Nicole lives in Chelsea. The fundraiser ended about half an hour after we posted this photo."

"Do you know any of Nicole's other close friends in New York? Or any family members?"

She shook her head. "I know her parents are dead and she has no brothers or sisters. She never mentioned any family. I invited her to my parents' house for Christmas dinner so she wouldn't be alone and we went to midnight mass together. Holidays are hard when you have no family."

"I appreciate you calling me back. If you think of anything or anyone else who might have useful information for Nicole, please let me know."

"I will. Tell her you talked to me and I wish her well. Should I call her?"

"Her phone was lost, but I'll tell her I spoke to you. I'll give her your number. She might want to talk to a friend."

Daniel disconnected. When he got home, he'd ask Hannah to calculate the probable date of conception for Nicole's baby. The timing might hold a clue.

CHAPTER TEN

Monday, October 24th, 2016

WHEN HANNAH GOT TO THE OFFICE MONDAY morning, she reviewed Nicole's medical record on her computer. Nicole must have had prenatal care somewhere. Hannah printed out a list of all the nearby L.A. County clinics and handed it to her receptionist.

"Could you call these and find out if Nicole Adler was a patient? Explain that she was admitted to Memorial, unconscious and pregnant after a serious accident, and we're trying to track down her prenatal records."

It didn't take long to get results. Nicole had been a patient at the USC County clinic. They emailed her records to Hannah later that afternoon.

The records were unremarkable but contained an address for an apartment in Hollywood and a cell phone number. Hannah hoped that the information would trigger some recall from Nicole. Gathering her purse and jacket, she headed for the hospital.

Nicole was exhausted. The physical therapist had arrived and took her through a series of exercises. He got more of a workout than she did because he had to move her arms and legs. She could only shrug her shoulders and slide her arms a few inches back and forth with the tiny amount of bicep function she still had. Her hands hung limp and useless.

The neurology team showed up in the late morning.

"Your vitals are stable and your head injury is healing. If things continue to look good, we can transfer you to the rehabilitation floor in a few days," Dr. Geller said.

"Will I be safe there?" Nicole asked.

Geller gave her a puzzled look.

"The detective told me that it wasn't an accident. Someone tried to kill me. She said she'd assign someone to guard me to prevent them from trying again."

"What?" Geller gave her a skeptical look.

"The detective left her card. Call her." *Did he think that her injuries had left her delusional?*

"I will. You should be as safe there as you are here," Geller assured her.

Shortly after lunch, a young police officer showed up.

"I'm Alberto Figueroa," he said. "Detective Abebe sent me here to make sure that no one enters your room without proper ID."

He looked tall and strong, and he was armed. Nicole breathed a sigh of relief.

Shortly afterward, a young woman introduced herself as the occupational therapist. She set up an iPad on a stand in front of Nicole and taught her how to operate it with voice control.

"I don't know what I can do with this," Nicole said. "If I have an email account, I don't remember how to access it and I don't recall the email address of anyone I might want to contact. All that information is on my phone and it's missing."

"Why don't we start with the newspaper?" the therapist suggested. "I understand you were living in New York. Would you like the New York Times?"

"I guess so."

"Tell Siri to open it for you."

The website appeared. "Oh my God, are we having an election?"

"In eight days."

"Fuchs is running for President? How did that happen? Never mind, just thinking about it makes me anxious. I don't want to read anymore. I'm tired."

The therapist gave her a sympathetic look. "If it makes you feel better, he's not the frontrunner. If the polls are right, we may finally have our first female president."

"Do you think America's ready for that?"

"I hope so. I'll leave the iPad. You might want to practice with it later."

"Ms. Adler, there's a doctor here to see you." The voice belonged to the nice policeman.

Nicole glanced up. Dr. Kline was at her bedside, smiling. Jeremy was in his bassinet, beside her bed.

"I've got some news for you," she said. "I managed to find your prenatal records from the County USC clinic and your Los Angeles address. You were living in Hollywood, just off Fountain Avenue."

Dr. Kline showed her a street view of a small apartment building.

"That looks vaguely familiar," Nicole said.

"If you give your permission, the detectives could go there and see if they can find any useful information. You might have a computer."

"That's a great idea. Any chance they could bring me something to wear other than these hospital gowns?"

"I'll see what I can do. I've also got your cell phone number."

"Should we call it?"

"I think not. The person who hit you might have your phone. Safer not to call it. But the police might be able to use the number to track the phone."

"Anything that would help identify the guy who ran me down is okay with me," Nicole said.

"I'll take care of it. I see you have a guard."

"The detectives think the hit and run was deliberate. They're protecting me until they catch whoever did it."

"Oh Nicole, I'm so sorry. You have enough to deal with right now."

"Thanks, Dr. Kline. Could you ask my nurse to come in? I fed Jeremy about two hours ago and I suspect he might be hungry again. I can't do it without help."

Hannah leaned over the bassinet and looked at the baby. "He's pretty adorable. I'm glad you've been able to feed him. Let me finish my exam and I'll send your nurse in. I'll come back and see you tomorrow morning."

CHAPTER ELEVEN

Tuesday, October 25th, 2016

DANIEL SCRIBBLED A NOTE ON A SCRAP OF PAPER and walked to Leila's desk.

"I've got something for you. Nicole Adler's Los Angeles address and cell phone number."

"Thanks, Sherlock. It wasn't listed. How'd you find it?"

"I didn't. Hannah called around to L.A. County prenatal clinics, looking for Nicole's pregnancy records, and managed to get them. You won't even need a warrant to search her apartment. She's happy to give permission, hoping you might find something that will help her remember."

"I owe you. Want to come with me tomorrow? We can stop by the hospital and get her written permission. Meantime, I'll track down her phone provider and put in a request for the records. Tell your wife I appreciate her help."

Daniel nodded. "Any word from forensics?"

He wanted to see if she would reciprocate and share her information.

Leila hesitated and then let out a breath. "This is confidential. They found fingerprints on the driver's side of the stolen truck and Nicole's blood on the front bumper. The prints belong to Felix Espinoza. He's a Nicaraguan gang member with a record. We're headed out to arrest him this afternoon. We'll book him for auto theft and see if we can get him to admit to driving during the hit-and-run. The only other fingerprints on the steering wheel belong to the legal owner."

"Good luck. I'm betting someone hired him to run Nicole down. I'd love to know who."

"I'll let you know when we're ready to interview him," Leila said. "You're welcome to watch."

"Thanks. I'd better get back to my desk." Daniel and Brenda were on duty today. Hopefully, no one would be murdered, and he'd be able to accompany Leila to Nicole's apartment tomorrow morning.

To Daniel's relief, there were no homicides on the West Side Monday night. He arrived at the station early the next day, interested in finding out how the arrest had proceeded.

"Things go okay yesterday?" Daniel asked.

Leila shook her head. "He was in his apartment, but someone got to him before we did. He had a bullet in the back of his head, execution style. Someone didn't want him to talk. The Hollenbeck division caught the case."

"Damn. Whoever is behind this is dangerous. I'd be worried about Nicole's safety."

"I am. I've got a 24/7 police guard on her, but I can't do that forever," Leila said. "There is some good news. Whoever did this took Espinoza's phone, but didn't look any further, because we found Nicole's purse and phone in his bedroom. The phone is passcode protected, but perhaps she might remember, or our IT guy can hack it."

Daniel smiled. "Izzy's very good at hacking. Why don't you leave the phone with him and we can ask Nicole when we see her. Anything in the purse that might be useful?"

"Yeah, her wallet and her keys. I delivered everything but the keys to forensics. We'll take the keys with us. That way we won't have to pick the lock to get in. We can't tell her the guy who ran her down is dead, but we can tell her we found her purse and phone."

"Maybe, between her apartment and the phone, we can figure out who wants her dead," Daniel said. "You ready to go?"

"Not yet. I need to pick up the written consent to search her apartment and deliver the phone to Izzy. I'll meet you in the parking lot."

Hannah was seated at the ICU nursing station, writing up her notes. Nicole was recovering nicely from her Caesarean section.

Daniel walked in, accompanied by a dark-skinned woman. "Hannah, I'm glad I caught you making rounds. This is Detective Leila Abebe. Leila, my wife, Dr. Hannah Kline."

"I hope your husband conveyed my thanks for the information. You've been very helpful," Leila said.

Hannah smiled. "He did, and I'm happy to help. I want to do anything I can to aid Nicole in recovering her memory."

Daniel hadn't mentioned that the new detective was gorgeous.

"We're planning to search Nicole's apartment today. We hope to find some clues about who attacked her," Leila said. "Would you mind staying a few minutes and being a witness? I need written permission from Nicole to search her apartment without a warrant."

"Sure."

The three of them entered Nicole's room. A nurse assistant was feeding her breakfast.

"Sorry for disturbing you," Leila said. "This is Detective Ross. We're planning to go to your apartment today and need your formal consent. I know you can't sign but you can agree verbally and I can have Dr. Kline and your nurse witness it."

"Can I read the consent?"

"Of course." Leila walked over and held the paper in front of Nicole.

"It's fine. I consent."

"I'll take pictures of your apartment while we're there and email them to Dr. Kline," Daniel said. "Maybe seeing it will help you remember something."

"That would be great," Nicole said. "Do you think you could bring me some comfortable clothes and pajamas? I'm transferring to rehabilitation in a few days and I'd rather not spend my life in hospital gowns."

"Of course," Leila said. "By the way, I have some good news. Your purse and phone were found. Forensics has them now but we'll get them back to you as soon as possible. I don't suppose you remember your password?"

"I do. It's 0316, my grandmother's birthday. She bought me my first cell phone."

"That will save us time," Daniel said. "We'll head over to your place and call you as soon as we've checked it out."

"Nicole, I'll see you tomorrow. You're recovering well," Hannah said.

"Will they let me see Jeremy once I'm in rehabilitation?"

"Of course they will."

Hannah and the detectives left the ICU.

"I'm worried that Nicole's getting attached to her baby," Hannah said.

"Isn't that a good thing?" Leila asked.

"Only if it turns out that she can keep him, but I'm not optimistic. Now, and for the foreseeable future, Nicole is going to need 24/7 care, the sort of care available only at a skilled nursing facility or at home if you are wealthy enough to afford it. She can't possibly care for this child."

"Maybe there's a rich husband in the picture," Daniel said, "and we can trace him."

Hannah sighed. "I'm not a believer in fairy tales. I think Nicole will be forced to give him up and suffer yet another heartbreaking blow. I'm so sad for her."

Daniel put an arm around her and drew her close. "That's why you are such a great doctor. You always care, and that's a gift."

CHAPTER TWELVE

Tuesday, October 25th 2016

Leila drove while Daniel phoned the station to give Izzy the code to Nicole's phone. Midmorning traffic was light, and it was less than half an hour later when they pulled up in front of Nicole's apartment building on a tree-lined street north of Fountain.

The building dated from the 1960s, with open garage space underneath, supported by columns. The parking spots were empty, the tenants probably at work. Leila pulled into a spot and shut off the engine. "Shall we?"

She shouldered her purse and opened the driver's side door. Daniel joined her. They climbed a set of steps and stood in front of a beige door, badly in need of a new coat of paint. They both put on latex gloves and shoe covers. Daniel doubted that the killer had been in the apartment, but should forensics be needed, he didn't want to mess anything up.

Leila took out the keys and opened the door. Daniel entered first. The apartment was tiny, no more than a studio, and meticulously neat. The carpet was gold shag and the refrigerator, an elderly model, was a shade of avocado. A convertible sofa faced a set of dresser drawers with a small flat-screen television on top. The kitchen was set against another wall and separated from the main room by a counter with one barstool. A rectangular table, being used as a desk, had a laptop and neat piles of paper sitting on it. A short hallway led to a bathroom and a closet.

"This shouldn't take long," Leila commented. "You check out the table and I'll hit the drawers and closets."

Daniel sat and booted up the computer. It was password-protected. He tried the four-digit code, but no luck. He slipped it into an evidence bag. Then he began scanning the papers.

"Most organized closets I've ever seen," Leila said. "I should hire her to arrange my apartment."

"Mostly bills here," Daniel said as he continued to flip through the pile. "Wait a second, I've found something. It's an adoption agreement with the Lady of Mercy Catholic adoption agency. She hasn't signed it yet, but it looks like she was planning to give up the baby."

"That certainly suggests the father wasn't about to step up. I wonder if he even knew she was pregnant." Leila said.

"Maybe not. We should probably talk to the agency and see if they know anything. Any luck in the drawers?"

"Not really. The few clothes she has were very neatly folded. I'm not finding a diary or written calendar or anything else useful. No meds in the medicine chest. No illegal drugs in the usual places. Nothing personal."

She walked over to the kitchen, opened the cabinets, and checked the refrigerator and freezer. "Definitely into healthy eating. We should throw out the food so it doesn't rot. She won't be coming home anytime soon."

Daniel finished one pile of papers and moved to the next one. These were mostly entertainment magazines, audition information and theater reviews. There was also a business card.

"Check this out," Daniel said. "Samantha Copeland, Attorney at Law."

"That's a familiar name," Leila said. "Isn't she one of those high-profile feminist attorneys who represent women suing powerful men who've abused them?"

"I think you're right. We should visit her. Are we done here?"

"Almost. I'm going to pack some clothes and toiletries for her before we leave. Why don't you clean out the refrigerator while I do that?"

Leila found a plastic garbage bag under the sink and handed it to Daniel. After emptying the refrigerator, Daniel took photos of the studio from several angles, along with a shot of the adoption papers and the business card. Then he slipped the papers into another evidence bag.

"I'm going to email these photos to you and Hannah," he said.

Leila looked up. "Why Hannah?"

"So she can show them to Nicole and see if anything triggers a memory."

"Showing Nicole those photos is my responsibility."

Daniel took a breath and reminded himself that she was new on the job. He understood why she might feel defensive. "One of the things I've had to learn over my years as a detective is that it is okay to accept help from people who aren't necessarily LAPD. I've had several cases in which Hannah's connections or insights have helped solve the crime. In this case, she sees Nicole daily and there's a relationship of trust because Hannah is Nicole's doctor. I think

Hannah can help her more easily than we can, and you can spend your time doing what you do best as a detective."

"What if Nicole remembers something and doesn't permit Hannah to tell us? Medical information is protected."

"Hannah would never breach medical confidentiality, but Nicole is anxious to find out who wants to kill her. If Hannah finds out anything pertinent, you'll be the first to know."

"Fine. Just remember, it's my case."

The two of them left the apartment, Daniel carrying the suitcase and the evidence, and Leila holding the garbage. Daniel put the suitcase in the trunk while Leila looked for the building dumpster. As he waited for her, he turned his ringtone back on and checked recent calls. There was one from Emily Harris. For a moment, the name was unfamiliar. Then he recalled that she was Nicole's other friend on Instagram.

"Miss Harris, this is Detective Ross returning your call."

"Brittany told me to get in touch with you. I'm so sorry to hear about Nicole. How is she doing?"

"She's making a slow recovery and there are still holes in her memory. She recognized the two of you on Instagram and I thought you might be able to tell me more about her. Anything I learn might help restore her memory of the past year. Do you have any idea why she left New York?"

"She said she'd have a better chance of acting if she was in Los Angeles because there were roles in movies and TV as well as theater. But I'm not sure that's the real reason. She'd been withdrawn and seemed depressed for several months before she left. Nicole was always a sunny personality and one of the smartest and nicest people I knew. I don't know if she was just tired of modeling, and felt unchallenged by what she was doing, or if she was lonely. She had no social life."

"She's a very attractive woman," Daniel said. "Any idea why she wasn't dating?"

"She's a romantic. I think she was looking for a soul mate, not a hookup. She's also Catholic and very religious. Nicole is the only person I know who goes to church every Sunday. The dating scene in New York is tough. Men want to sleep with you first, before deciding if you're worth their time. Nicole wasn't up for that. I don't think she's even on any of the dating apps. Maybe she thought she would meet the love of her life at church."

"When was the last time you saw or spoke to her?"

"Brittany and I took her out for dinner a few days before she left for Los Angeles. I called several times after she left and we chatted, but she never initiated any calls to me. So, after a few months, I stopped. Last I heard, she was working at some health food restaurant as a waitress. Not a great job for a smart woman with a college degree."

"Do you recall the name of the restaurant?"

"Sorry, I don't. Is there anything else you want to know?"

"Not at the moment, but if you don't mind, I'll call you if I have more questions. Thanks for your help." Daniel ended the call as Leila returned and opened the car door.

"I guess we're going back to the station," she said.

"I have a better idea. How about we go to church?"

CHAPTER THIRTEEN

Tuesday, October 25th 2016

Saint Marten's, the closest Catholic church to Nicole's apartment, was on Sunset Boulevard. It was a 1920s Spanish Revival-style building, painted a light shade of peach and trimmed with pale turquoise.

Daniel held the heavy door open for Leila. The church interior was cool and empty, scented with incense, and dimly lit. They walked through the nave to the sanctuary, pausing to admire the art and architecture.

"Anybody here?" Leila asked loudly.

"Can I help you?" A tall, slim priest, dressed in standard black clothing with a white collar, appeared from the left end of the sanctuary. He was middle-aged, with features that suggested a Latino background, and a thick head of black hair, peppered with gray.

"I'm Father Gomez."

"We're LAPD detectives, Abebe and Ross," Leila said. "Sorry to disturb you, Father, but we're seeking information about a young woman we think might be one of your parishioners, Nicole Adler."

"Is Nicole in trouble?"

"She was the victim of a hit-and-run on Friday night. The injuries resulted in substantial amnesia. We are seeking out people who knew her and might be able to help her fill in some gaps. A friend of hers from New York told us she was a devout Catholic. We thought perhaps there might be a priest here who knew her."

"I'm so sorry to hear that," Father Gomez said. "What about her baby?"

"He's fine," Daniel said. "But Nicole is paralyzed and won't be able to care for the baby alone. We were hoping to find any family members who might be able to help her."

The priest shook his head. "She has no living family, except for a grandmother in a nursing home."

"What about the baby's father?" Leila asked.

"What I know about him is under the seal of the confessional."

"We would never expect you to break that seal, Father," Leila assured him.

"Would you be willing to visit Nicole at Memorial Hospital?" Daniel asked. Perhaps seeing you will help her to remember and make decisions about the baby's care. She's in the neurosurgical ICU."

"Of course I will," Father Gomez said. "I'll go this afternoon. Thank you for telling me. Nicole will need the comfort of her faith to help her through this crisis."

Leila reached into her purse and handed the priest her card. "If you learn anything that might help us find who did this to her, please call me."

The two of them left the church.

"Good thinking," Leila said. "I'll bet he knows what we want to know."

"I agree. Where to now?"

Leila looked at her watch. "I'm starving. How about lunch and then a visit to that lawyer?"

Daniel nodded and entered the address on the card into Google Maps. "This is interesting. Her office is on Wilshire, only two blocks from where Nicole was run down."

"Could Nicole have been meeting with the attorney Friday night?"

"I guess we'll find out."

Nicole had just finished lunch when there was a knock on the door and the young police officer poked his head in. "There's someone to see you, Miss Adler. A priest."

The tall, dark-haired man in black looked familiar.

"May I come in?"

"Did they send you to give me last rites?"

"No, of course not, Nicole. I'm Father Gomez from St. Marten's, your church. I just found out what happened to you. I wanted to see if I could offer some comfort."

"I'll leave you two to talk privately," the nurse said, setting Nicole's tray on a side table and leaving the room. The priest sat down in the chair near the head of her bed.

"It's okay for you to leave," Nicole said to the police officer.

"I'll be right outside if you need me."

"I don't have any specific memory of you," Nicole said to the priest, "just a feeling that you're someone I can trust."

"Perhaps we could pray together for your recovery."

"It's going to take more than prayers to fix me, Father. How could God allow this to happen to me and to Jeremy?"

"Jeremy?"

"My son. They delivered him Friday night."

"You mustn't lose faith, Nicole. God does things for a reason, even though we may not understand His reasons at the time. He knows more and sees more than we do. And He doesn't present us with challenges we can't handle."

"Well, I have no idea how to handle this challenge," Nicole said.

"With God's help, my child. Keep your faith close and it will comfort you."

"It hasn't helped me so far. God must have been too busy to pay attention when I was run over. Either that or this is my punishment for doing something unforgivable. Did I ever go to confession, Father?"

"Every week. You are extremely devout and strong in your faith. That's why I know you will be able to handle this."

"Really? Did God tell you how I'm going to be able to raise Jeremy all by myself when I'm paralyzed from the neck down?"

The priest shook his head.

It was so easy for him to talk in platitudes. He never had to nurse a baby he couldn't even hold. Had she been so naïve as to believe that God would take care of her?

"Tell me, Father, in my confessions, did I ever tell you who Jeremy's father was? Is he someone who would step up and take care of the two of us?"

"You did tell me, but I'm afraid the father won't be the answer to your problem."

"Enlighten me. I need to know."

"It's a painful story," Father Gomez said. "Perhaps we should wait until you are stronger to revisit it."

"You said you wanted to help."

"I do."

"Then I need your information. Please, Father, I have to know now."

CHAPTER FOURTEEN

Tuesday, October 25th, 2016

AFTER A QUICK LUNCH AT A HOLE-IN-THE-WALL THAI place on Beverly Boulevard, Daniel called the attorney's office to schedule an appointment, only to be told that Samantha Copeland was in court that afternoon.

"I can schedule you in for tomorrow morning, Detective," the receptionist said.

Daniel coordinated calendars with Leila and made an appointment for 11:00 a.m., the next day.

"Back to the station?" he asked.

She nodded.

When Daniel walked in, he saw Brenda at her desk.

"Hey, Daniel. What's up?"

"Have you met our new detective, Leila Abebe?" Daniel asked.

Brenda stood up and shook hands. "I haven't. Are you with homicide?"

"No. I'm working on a hit-and-run at the moment. Daniel's been helping out."

"Welcome to the station. Always happy to have an extra pair of hands."

Leila nodded and headed to her desk.

"So, Daniel? Are you replacing me with another woman?" Brenda asked.

He laughed. "Not a chance. I don't think Leila wants my help. She's very protective about her case, but I outrank her so she tolerates me."

"Cut her some slack. She's new, a woman and black. No doubt she's been hassled and underestimated, and has reason to be suspicious of you."

"You're right. But it would be nice if I could stop walking on eggs around her."

"I can understand that. Update me on the case. We haven't had a new murder in a while. I've been mired in paperwork. I'm getting bored."

CHAPTER FIFTEEN

Wednesday, October 26, 2016

Hannah got up early on Wednesday morning, to give herself some extra time with Nicole when she did rounds. Daniel had brought a small duffel bag with comfortable clothes and pajamas home, and had reviewed his photographs with Hannah the previous night.

"It looks as if she intended to give her baby up for adoption," Hannah said. "Although, she hasn't signed the paperwork. Maybe she was waiting to see how she felt after he was born."

Daniel shrugged. "You know she'll have to. There's no way she can care for him. She can't care for herself. What kind of future do you see for her?"

"She'll be stuck in a nursing home with 24/7 caregivers who do a lousy job. She'll get bedsores, urinary tract infections and pneumonia, and be in and out of the hospital until she dies. If she were wealthy and had a loving family, she might be able to live in her home with round-the-clock aides, but that's not happening. I hate this!"

Daniel hugged her. "I know you do.

"I wish there was something I could do to make her feel better."

"Knowing someone cares makes her feel better."

It was 7:00 a.m., and change of shift time, when Hannah entered the ICU. Nicole was awake but drowsy.

"Hi there."

"You're early, Dr. Kline."

"I brought you the clothes the detectives packed for you and a few photos of your apartment. I wanted some extra time before the nurses start your morning routine."

Hannah put the duffel bag on a side table and took out her phone. She adjusted Nicole to a sitting position and stood next to her, swiping through the pictures.

"What a boring apartment," Nicole said. "Do I live there?"

"You do. It does seem impersonal. Maybe you were too busy to decorate."

"Or too stressed and depressed."

"Have you remembered something more?" Hannah asked.

"Not exactly. I had a visit yesterday from my priest. He told me everything I revealed to him in confession. Now I know who the father is and why I moved here from New York."

"Oh! Is there anything you feel comfortable sharing?"

Nicole hesitated, then took a deep breath. "I was raped and I left because I needed to start a new life, somewhere where no one knew me, or would judge me, or try to make my decisions for me."

Hannah connected the dots. Nicole was a religious Catholic. Abortion was not an option for her. She probably felt guilty about being raped. Her friends would have urged her to terminate.

"Do you know the identity of the man who raped you?" Hannah asked.

"I don't know his name. The only good thing about this brain injury is that I can't remember anything about the rape. All I know from my priest is that it happened after that fundraiser I posted on Instagram."

"You had a strongly negative reaction to a photo of a man in the background. Could it have been him?" Hannah reviewed the photos on her phone and found the one she was looking for.

Nicole shuddered. "Please put it away. I don't want to see his face again."

"Is there any way he might have discovered you were pregnant?"

"I have no idea. I don't think I ever saw him again. How could I have fallen in love with the baby of my rapist?"

Hannah reached over and touched Nicole's shoulder, knowing that she had sensation there and could feel a comforting hand.

"Jeremy is innocent and half his genetic inheritance is from you. Mothers fall in love with their babies all the time. It's how nature makes sure someone feeds and takes care of helpless infants."

"I told the nurses yesterday to stop bringing him and to give me something to dry up my milk. I can't nurse him and I can't keep him."

"I'm so sorry, Nicole. Do I have your permission to share this information with the detectives? They should be able to identify the man."

"What for? I don't want to file charges because I don't want him to know about Jeremy. What if he files for custody?"

"We don't know who this guy is, or what he might stand to lose if word of the rape and pregnancy became public. He might be someone who's capable of killing both of you."

"In that case," Nicole said, "I guess you'd better phone the detectives."

"That explains a great deal. I guess my expedition to that church paid dividends. Thank you, sweetheart." Daniel disconnected Hannah's call.

"Breakthrough?" Brenda asked.

"Maybe."

"Do tell."

"I should tell Leila first," Daniel said.

He walked over to Leila's desk, pulled out a chair, and sat.

"I've got a lead."

Leila raised an eyebrow.

"Hannah made rounds this morning. Our priest saw Nicole yesterday and refreshed her memory from her confessions. She was raped by a man at that Fuchs fundraiser and became pregnant. She doesn't remember his name, but I'm sure Izzy can do some facial recognition on the photos and find out."

"That sounds like major progress." Leila glanced at her watch. "We need to leave soon to see the lawyer. Let's give Izzy the photo and get going."

Samantha Copeland's office was in a high rise, around the corner from the scene of the accident. Copeland and Associates was on the top floor. The elevator deposited them in a lushly carpeted reception area presided over by an attractive receptionist. She asked them to be seated and escorted them to a large corner office a few minutes later.

"Ms. Copeland is just finishing up in the conference room. Can I get you some coffee or tea?"

"No thank you," Leila said.

"Then make yourselves comfortable."

Daniel admired the view north to the hills and then joined Leila, seated on one of two comfortable white leather chairs. The office was pristine, with a large black marble desk containing only a computer monitor and an elegant set of pens. Anything as crass as a file or book was discretely hidden behind white lacquer cabinets. The only personal touches were an edgy collection of modern art and a large glass vase of red roses.

"Detectives." Samantha Copeland entered the room.

They stood up to shake hands and introduce themselves.

"Thank you for seeing us," Daniel said.

The attorney wasn't quite what he expected. He'd probably been watching too many episodes of *The Good Wife*. She was short and squat, wearing a navy blue suit with a tight jacket and straight skirt that did not flatter her. He guessed she was in her fifties with a round face, jowls, and wrinkles. Her sandy hair, streaked with gray, was cut short and her outfit included sensible shoes and no jewelry.

"How can I help you?"

"We are investigating an attempted murder of a pregnant woman named Nicole Adler. She was the victim of a hit-and-run Friday night, around the corner from your office. Your card was found in her purse."

Copeland's jaw dropped. "Oh my God. How badly was she hurt?"

"Very badly. She was left a quadriplegic. She underwent surgery, delivered the baby, and is recovering in the ICU at Memorial Hospital.

Copeland shook her head. "What a horrible accident. She was here Friday night, meeting with me about a possible lawsuit. She must have been walking back to her car when it happened."

"It doesn't appear to have been an accident. We have evidence that the driver deliberately targeted her. We're trying to figure out who might have wanted her dead."

"Any chance you could tell us about the lawsuit?" Daniel asked. "The person she's suing may have had a motive."

"You know I can't. Attorney-client privilege. Didn't Nicole tell you about it?"

Daniel sighed. "She couldn't. She has amnesia from a brain injury sustained when her head hit the ground. Most of the previous year is a blank. She couldn't even remember who the baby's father is."

From the expression on the attorney's face, Daniel could tell he'd hit a nerve and she was putting the pieces together.

"Ms. Copeland," Leila said, "we need your help. Would you be willing to visit Nicole in the Neurosurgical ICU with us? Perhaps seeing you might trigger a memory. Even if it doesn't, she could give you permission to share what you know."

"Of course. I'm free later this afternoon." She looked at her watch. "I could meet you in the hospital lobby at four o'clock."

"We appreciate it," Daniel said. "We won't take up any more of your time."

Daniel's phone rang as they reached their car. It was Izzy.

"Any luck?"

"You bet. Facial recognition identified him quickly. The guy's been on TV quite a lot. His name is Kenneth Palmer."

"I know that name."

"You should. He's a big Texas oilman and mega-donor to the Fuchs campaign. His name has been mentioned as a possible Secretary of Energy, or White House Chief of Staff, should Fuchs win the presidential election. Does this help?"

"If Palmer is the rapist, it certainly provides a motive for keeping Nicole quiet. Proving that connection, however, is not going to be easy. Even if we link him to the baby, genetically, proving that it was rape, when the victim has no memory of the event, is going to be difficult."

CHAPTER SIXTEEN

Wednesday, October 26th 2016

DETECTIVE ABEBE KNOCKED ON THE DOOR TO Nicole's ICU room. Nicole was alone, sitting in a chair, her limp hands supported by a pillow on her lap.

"Hello Detective. Any news?"

"Yes. I have someone I would like you to meet."

Detective Ross came through the door next, accompanied by a short, squat, gray-haired woman.

"This is attorney Samantha Copeland," he said. "Do you remember her at all?"

Nicole stared at the attorney, her eyes slowly examining her face. "I feel like I know you but I don't remember who you are."

"May I sit?" Samantha asked.

Nicole nodded.

Samantha seated herself on the edge of the bed, across from Nicole.

"You and I met Friday night, just before your accident.

My office is two blocks from where it happened. Would you like to continue this conversation in private?"

"No need. The detectives should hear any information you have. Do you know anything that might help identify the person responsible for destroying my life?"

The attorney nodded. "You came to Los Angeles after having been raped and impregnated at a Fuchs fundraiser in New York. You didn't know the identity of the man who raped you until a few days before you came to see me. That's when you saw him on television, identified as Kenneth Palmer. He's a Fuchs advisor and he's being considered for a high-level administrative job in the White House, should Fuchs win the election for President."

"I can't believe I forgot all of that. After the accident, I had no idea who had fathered my baby. I thought I was still in New York. I don't even remember the fundraiser."

"You came to see me because you wanted to explore filing charges against Kenneth Palmer and publicizing the rape accusation. You didn't think a rapist should be appointed to a position of power. Your current amnesia, unfortunately, makes a public lawsuit very difficult."

"The baby's DNA could prove paternity," Leila said.

"It would. But the defense would just claim consensual sex, and without Nicole having told anyone or filed a report at the time, it would be very hard to prove otherwise."

"Of course. Rape is always the woman's fault anyway, isn't it? She looked too sexy. She came onto him. She'd slept with other men and was a whore!" Nicole turned to Detective Abebe. "Do you think this Kenneth Palmer is responsible for the hit and run?"

"He's the only person we've identified so far with a motive, but suspecting he was behind the hit-and-run is vastly different from proving that he hired someone to try to kill you. That's going to be challenging. At least we have a direction to investigate now."

"Even if I could remember," Nicole said, "I'm not sure I want to file charges."

"Why not?" Samantha asked.

"What if he comes after my son? What if he wants custody?"

"Are you planning to keep your son?" Leila asked.

"I can't. I mean, look at me. I can't even feed or take care of myself. How can I take care of a baby? But I want him to be in a loving home, not living with a rapist. His well-being is more important to me than putting that man in jail."

"I understand." Samantha rose and took a card from her purse, leaving it on the pillow next to Nicole's hands. "I know this is a lot to process and you need time to think it through. If you decide you need an attorney, I'm happy to help you, pro bono, with whatever you need. What happened to you is despicable. You and your son deserve some justice."

Daniel followed Samantha out of the ICU and caught up to her at the elevator. "Are you certain you can't make a rape charge stick?"

She punched the button for the elevator hard, her face tight. "It would be a challenge in criminal court, but I'm contemplating some other options. I thought I'd give Nicole a few days to think things over and visit her again. This whole story infuriates me, and I'm awesome in court when I am truly pissed off at the defendant. Seeing Nicole in her current condition almost brought me to tears. Imagine how it would affect a jury." The elevator doors opened and she got in, still seething. Daniel found himself hoping she got her day in court. If anyone could convince a jury to put Palmer away for the rest of his life, it would be Attorney Samantha Copeland.

Back at the station, Leila suggested a strategy session to decide how to proceed.

"I'd like to include Brenda, my partner if that's okay with you," Daniel said. "She's very smart and might come up with ideas we don't think of. I also think that Izzy would be helpful. He's a genius at computer data."

"No problem," Leila said. This case was clearly beyond a routine hit-and-run that could be handled by one detective. She needed a team, but she also needed to make it clear to everyone that she, not Daniel, was in charge.

The four of them moved to a conference room and Leila set up a whiteboard.

"Here's the situation as I see it," Leila said. "Nicole Adler was attacked deliberately by a gang member in a stolen car, who ostensibly had no connection to her and no motive for killing her. That suggests a paid hit."

"Agreed," Daniel said. "Especially since the gang member was murdered shortly thereafter. Someone went to great lengths to cover his tracks."

Leila continued. "So far, the only person we've been able to identify with a motive is Kenneth Palmer. He can't afford to be exposed as a rapist with an illegitimate child if Fuchs wins next week and Palmer is nominated for a cabinet position."

"That assumes that he knows Nicole was pregnant. That's a pretty big assumption. He may not have even known her name," Brenda said. "He would have had to identify her and perhaps have hired someone to follow her to Los Angeles."

"Either he has a trusted staff person who is his "fixer" or he hired a private detective agency. That sounds like a place to start," Izzy said. "I suggest you check with the head of the agency that employed Nicole to see if anyone tried to get in touch with her. I'll do a deep dive into Palmer's staff and see if I can identify someone who might have flown to L.A. recently."

"I'll call the agency. I've spoken to them before. It also would help to get phone records for Palmer and any of his staff we might suspect," Daniel said.

"Has there been any progress identifying the person who killed the driver?" Brenda asked.

"Hollenbeck caught that murder case. I'll see what I can find out," Leila said.

"Let's keep in mind that just because Kenneth Palmer is a viable suspect, doesn't mean he was responsible. We have to connect a lot of dots to prove him guilty. Nicole may have met someone else she doesn't remember who has a grudge," Brenda suggested. "Have we checked out her workplace?"

"Not yet," Leila said.

"I volunteer," Brenda said.

"One more thing we need to remember," Leila said. "This was an attempted murder that failed. The killer may well try again. We need to keep Nicole protected."

CHAPTER SEVENTEEN

Thursday, October 27th, 2016

HANNAH FINISHED HER 7:30 A.M. LAPAROSCOPIC surgery, dictated her operative report, and wrote her orders. Checking her watch, she decided she still had plenty of time to make rounds, and to grab breakfast at the hospital coffee shop. On her way, she had an urge to stop in the nursery.

The pediatric nurses were busy feeding and burping babies. They acknowledged her with a wave and a "Hi!" and returned to their duties. Hannah meandered along the aisle of bassinets until she came to Jeremy's. He was awake and alert and had managed to free both his arms from the blanket swaddling him. He grabbed her finger with his hand and looked at her with his large blue eyes. She leaned over and picked him up.

He had that irresistible new baby smell of powder and milk, the softest skin, and wispy hair. She held him on her shoulder and walked with him around the nursery.

"Has he been fed?" she asked the nurse.

"Not yet."

"I'll do it," Hannah offered. "I've got time and I'm taking care of his mother."

The nurse handed her a bottle. "What a tragedy."

Hannah nodded, seating herself in a rocking chair and giving Jeremy a bottle. He swallowed hungrily, his little hands touching hers. It broke her heart. What was going to happen to him? Would he find a loving family or be stuck in an institution? Would he be handed off to a series of foster parents who were only doing it for the money? Was there any way she could help Nicole keep him or adopt him herself? He was adorable.

She let him finish his bottle and burped him, replacing him in his bassinet. She needed to make rounds and stop fantasizing about adoption. They weren't ready. It hadn't been that long since her miscarriage. She had more embryos to implant. Did she want another child? Did they have the time and energy to expand their family? Was she thinking with her head or her hormones? What would Daniel say about all this?

Daniel looked through the contacts on his phone until he found the New York Star Model Agency. He called and asked for the manager.

"Hello, Detective. Any news about Nicole? We've all been concerned about her."

"She's recovering slowly," Daniel answered. "She has a long way to go."

"Please tell her that we're all thinking about her. How can I help you?"

"I'm wondering if anyone reached out to you after Nicole moved, trying to get in touch with her?"

"Now that you mention it, there was a man who called shortly after Nicole moved to Los Angeles. He wanted to contact the blonde model who attended a Fuchs fundraiser in January. He didn't recall her name but he said he was impressed with her. He wanted to invite her to attend an even more exclusive event."

"What did you tell him?"

"I said I knew who he meant, but she no longer worked for us. I told him she moved out of town. He wanted her email and phone number, but I said it was confidential. If one of our models wants to share personal information she can, but we maintain their privacy in the agency."

"Good to know," Daniel said. "Unfortunately with social media, few things are confidential these days. Did the caller give you his name?"

"He may have, but I don't remember. I'm sorry."

"That would have been back in March, right?"

"Yes, I believe so."

"Would you happen to have a copy of your March phone bill? It would save me time with the phone company."

"I'll have my secretary scan it. She can email it to you," Amber said. "I just need your email address."

Daniel complied and signed off. Feeling frustrated, he grabbed two doughnuts and a cup of black coffee from the station kitchen and returned to his desk. Brenda was seated at hers.

"Anything of interest?" she asked.

Daniel shrugged. "A man was looking for Nicole. I'm betting on Palmer. I should have some phone records soon."

"I don't suppose you know the restaurant where Nicole was employed?"

"Not off the top of my head, but there were some pay

stubs in the papers I took from her desk. I'll retrieve them from Evidence."

"Good. I thought I'd go there before they get busy for lunch. Want to come? We could check out the food if you don't spoil your appetite with more doughnuts."

"Yeah. I always like your company when I'm feeling stuck and frustrated."

"I'm not sure if that was meant to be a compliment," Brenda said, reaching for Daniel's uneaten second doughnut.

"Believe me, it is. I certainly don't want to vent to Leila."

Leila stood in front of her closet, scanning the possibilities. She had already decided that her best chance of getting information on the Espinoza murder was to show up at the Hollenbeck LAPD station in person. Wade Calloway, the detective who'd caught the case, was one of her least favorite people and she doubted he'd take her call.

She pushed aside her jeans and athletic wear and concentrated on her pantsuits, settling for dark brown, a shade lighter than her skin, and an ivory cotton blouse. Brown ankle boots completed the outfit, and she drew her hair back into a sleek twist. No jewelry.

The station was on First Street; an unassuming beige brick building, punctuated by narrow horizontal windows. Only the glass entrance gave the building any class. She opened the door and walked up to the front desk.

"Can I help you, Ma'am?"

She pulled her badge out of her jacket pocket. "Detective Abebe from West LA. I'm looking for Detective Calloway. He in?"

"Yes Ma'am, uh, Detective. Shall I call him for you?"

"No need. I know the way. I was stationed here not too long ago."

He smiled at her and opened the door to the back offices. She followed the well-worn path to the large workspace shared by the detectives and headed to Calloway's cubicle. She spotted the back of his head with its sparse graying hair and sweating scalp, and noted the rolls of fat distending the sides of his gray polo shirt. His computer monitor was live and she noticed his sausage-like fingers busily typing.

"Detective Calloway," she said.

Callaway spun around. "Well, look who's here. Howdy, Princess. You bored already at West L.A. with all the Brentwood types?"

"Not at all. I'm here because we have a case that overlaps one of yours, and I thought the polite thing would be to discuss it in person." Leila pulled up a chair and sat down opposite him without waiting for an invitation.

"And what case would that be?"

"The murder of Felix Espinoza. He was driving a car that hit and severely wounded a pregnant woman. It was clear from the security tapes that he deliberately accelerated when she was crossing the street. We think it was a murder for hire. The fact that Espinoza was taken out immediately after suggests we're right. Any chance you have a clue as to who killed him?"

Calloway leaned back, placed his hands on his protuberant abdomen, and grinned at her. "Honey, we have the perp in lockup."

Leila dug her nails into her palms and kept her face blank. Calloway was one of the reasons she was happy to have been transferred. "No kidding. Do tell. How'd you identify him and who is he?"

"I have informants in all the gangs in this neighborhood. The killer is a fellow gang member named Orlando Sanchez. These guys are not too bright. He kept the gun he used, and the bullet in Espinoza's head was a match."

"They probably don't watch CSI," Leila commented. "Sounds like a slam dunk in court. Any chance I could question him with you?"

Calloway licked his lips. "Sure, Princess, but you're going to owe me one."

Leila was sure she knew what he had in mind. It might be wise to give his imagination free rein.

She forced a smile onto her face. "I'm a big fan of cops helping each other out."

CHAPTER EIGHTEEN

Thursday, October 27th, 2016

THE RESTAURANT'S NAME WAS STARLIGHT AND IT was in Silver Lake, in a white clapboard bungalow with blue trim. A front patio with seating, hanging plants and a fountain was currently occupied by a middle-aged woman nursing a mug of coffee and reading a hardback book.

Daniel and Brenda walked toward the front door.

"We aren't open yet," the woman said, looking up. "If you're here for lunch, you're welcome to sit at a patio table."

The woman had a kind face, devoid of makeup, and displayed a pattern of wrinkles around her eyes when she smiled. She had thick black hair with gray streaks and wore faded jeans, sandals and a brightly embroidered Guatemalan huipil.

"We're here to talk to the manager," Daniel said.

"That's me. Carolina Cordova."

"I'm Detective Ross of the LAPD," Daniel said, removing his badge from his pocket. "This is Detective Jordan. We're here about one of your employees, Nicole Adler."

A look of alarm crossed her face. "Has something happened to Nicole?"

"When did you last see her?" Daniel asked.

"On Friday. It was her last day at work before her maternity leave. Is the baby okay?"

"The baby's fine," Brenda said. "But Nicole was the victim of a hit-and-run. She was badly injured."

"Oh my God! Please, tell me why you're here."

Daniel pulled out a chair, motioned for Brenda to sit, and then fetched one for himself. "Nicole is hospitalized at Memorial Hospital. She survived the hit but she's going to have a difficult recovery. We're here because she has memory loss and we're trying to fill in whatever we can about her life. Was she involved with anyone who might have wished to harm her?"

Carolina shook her head. "Nicole is one of the nicest people I've ever worked with. Her co-workers loved her. Regular customers would come in and ask for her table. She was kind and generous to everyone. I can't imagine that anyone would want to hurt her."

"Did she have a boyfriend?" Brenda asked.

"Not in the sense you mean. She was closest to Brian Lewis, one of our waiters, but he's gay. They were just good friends. And being very pregnant, she didn't date."

"Did she talk to you about her plans for the baby?" Daniel said.

"She was struggling," Carolina said. "She'd spoken with a Catholic adoption agency but was ambivalent about giving the child away. She was also scared that she couldn't manage as a single mother. I raised two kids by myself after my husband split, so I know a man is no guarantee of parental help. No offense intended."

"No offense taken," Daniel said. "Did she have anyone here she could rely on for help?"

"I promised to help her find daycare when she was ready to come back to work, and I think any of us would have helped her in an emergency, but there was no loving mother or grandmother or extended family. She was very much on her own. I suggested she give herself time with the baby to see how she felt before making a final decision."

"Is Mr. Lewis working today?" Daniel asked. "I'd like to talk to him."

"He should be in shortly," Carolina said. "Can we visit her at the hospital?"

"I think so," Daniel said. "She's awake and able to make conversation. I think she'd enjoy having visitors but don't be upset if she doesn't remember you."

"I won't be. I just want her to know that she has friends who care about her and that she's not alone."

Daniel smiled. "I can't think of anything she needs more, right now."

Nicole finished breakfast and awaited the arrival of the neurology team. She was feeling reasonably pain-free and needed to know her next steps.

Dr. Geller entered her room, trailed by his residents and medical students. By now, she was familiar with his exam as he checked her incisions, eye movements, reflexes and senses. Nothing seemed to have changed, as far as she could tell.

"You're stable," he said. "I think we can transfer you to the rehabilitation floor. It's time to do the hard work of getting better."

"Am I going to get better?" she asked.

"They will help you function as well as you possibly can, given your limitations, and physical improvement in your condition is possible. I fully expect some of your memory to return."

Nicole didn't bother asking any more questions. Geller was always evasive about her prognosis. Maybe the physician in the rehabilitation department would be more forthcoming.

By early afternoon she had been transferred to a bed on an upper floor. The room was much larger than her ICU cubicle and had windows facing north to the hills. The orderlies lifted her to her bed, raised her back so she was in a sitting position, and stabilized her arms with pillows. As she settled in, a young woman in a white coat entered the room.

"Welcome to the rehabilitation center. I'm Doctor Ito and I'll be taking care of you."

Her smile was warm and genuine, her thick black hair beautiful and shiny. Nicole's anxiety subsided. Maybe this was a person she could talk to.

"Thank you. They didn't tell me anything about what you do in rehabilitation for someone like me who can't move anything. I assume aerobics are out of the question."

Dr. Ito laughed. "I'm afraid so, but we are going to keep you very busy for the next few months. Shall I review the schedule and activities for you?"

"Please."

"Our occupational therapist will be helping you to use your voice to connect with the outside world. We will teach you to replace many functions you do with your hands with voice-activated software."

"I was an actress and a model before this happened. I wasn't famous or anything. I mostly did off-Broadway small theater and catalog modeling, but I was earning a living. There isn't much demand for quadriplegic models. Will your occupational therapist help me find a new occupation?"

"That's part of the therapy. She'll work with you to explore options for earning money that you can do with your new skills. We'll also have our social worker help you apply for Social Security and Medicare Disability payments so you will have medical insurance and an income."

"What else is on the schedule?"

"Our physical therapist will give you range of motion exercises for your arms, hands and legs. You will get special gloves to wear with open fingertips, to keep your hands from curling up."

"What difference does it make if I can't use them to feed myself or wipe myself after I have a bowel movement?"

"I'm getting to that." Dr. Ito pulled up a chair and sat down. "We've been making some real progress. I'm planning to start you on electrostimulation. We stimulate the nerves below the site of your injury, using electrodes on your skin. Stimulating those nerves combined with intensive training can restore some of your hand and arm function. Eventually, you may be able to eat by yourself."

"Now that's an incentive." She hated being fed, and it wasn't just the hospital food. Maybe it wasn't hopeless after all.

"Did they tell you I just had a baby? What about him? Can he visit me here?"

"He can, but truthfully, the hospital can't keep him for

the length of time you will be here. We can help you make other arrangements, like foster care, until you're ready to leave. That's something you can discuss with our social worker."

Foster care. The very thought of Jeremy being dependent on the foster care system terrified her. Maybe Dr. Kline would know of a better alternative. She'd ask her tomorrow when she made rounds. She might also have an update on the investigation. Nicole suspected that Dr. Kline had an inside source at the LAPD.

CHAPTER NINETEEN

Thursday, October 27th, 2016

LEILA FOLLOWED DETECTIVE CALLOWAY TO THE station interview room where Orlando Sanchez, dressed in prison garb, his hands cuffed, sat on one side of a scuffed table.

The two of them sat down opposite Sanchez and Calloway turned on the recorder. He read Sanchez his rights, introduced Leila, and sat back, giving her the go-ahead to proceed.

"Hello, Mr. Sanchez. I'm Detective Abebe. I have a few questions for you about Felix Espinoza."

Sanchez said nothing, his face a blank.

"You knew Mr. Espinoza?"

Sanchez shrugged. "I seen him around the neighborhood."

"Then maybe you can help me, and I can help you."

"I don't need your help."

Calloway leaned forward. "Yes, you do, asshole. The bullet in Espinoza's head is a match for the gun in your apartment. You wanna spend the rest of your life in Pelican Bay or you wanna talk to the lady? You help us, we talk to the DA about getting you a lighter sentence."

Calloway had always been very good at doing bad cop.

Leila turned to her fellow detective. "No need to bully, Detective Callaway. Mr. Sanchez is smart enough to know how things work around here."

She turned back to Sanchez.

"Your fellow gang member was the driver in a hit-and-run. He hit a pregnant lady, deliberately. We figure, murder for hire, and that Espinoza's murder was just tying up loose ends."

"What's that got to do with me?" Sanchez kept his face expressionless but beads of sweat were breaking out over his forehead. Leila could see his knee vibrating with tension.

"We want to know who hired Espinoza."

"How would I know that?"

Leila sat back and let the silence build. She watched a drop of sweat make its way down Sanchez's prominent nose. "We think it's the same guy who hired you. You want our help, you tell us his name. But if you want to go to prison for something he's responsible for, that's fine with us."

"He didn't tell me his fucking name!" Sanchez shouted, slamming his fists on the table.

"No need to yell, Mr. Sanchez," Leila said, smiling. Did he realize he'd just confessed? "Just tell me how you got the job and I'll visit the DA on your behalf."

"Got a call on Sunday offering me fifty grand to do the job, half up front and the rest after the hit. The guy didn't tell me his name. I didn't think it was real until a bag of cash was left in a locker at Union Station on Monday, and the key appeared in my mailbox."

"So you did the job?" Leila asked.

"Monday night. Tuesday there was a note in my box that said I should check my locker. The rest of the cash was there."

"He called you on your cell?"

Sanchez nodded.

"He speak English or Spanish?"

"Spanish."

"How'd he get your number?" Calloway asked.

Sanchez shrugged. "Hell if I know."

"Thank you, Mr. Sanchez," Leila said. "I have one more question. Where's the cash now?"

"How would I know? Ask him," he said, nodding his head at Calloway.

Calloway rolled his eyes. "We got it. Asshole had it in his apartment."

They wrapped up the interrogation and left the room.

"Not bad, Princess," Calloway said.

"High praise, coming from you."

"We got us some loose ends someone may be looking to tie up," he said. "You have to have gang connections to get Sanchez's name and number."

"Not to mention police connections to find out so quickly that the job was done," Leila said.

"Good point."

"You got Sanchez's phone in evidence?" Leila asked.

Calloway nodded.

"Can I download the contents and send it to our AI guy in West LA?"

"As long as you share anything you track down."

"Goes without saying," Leila said. "Let's head over to Evidence."

She would email the download to Izzy and ask him to check out the Sunday night calls and trace them. It would be useful to have that information before the afternoon briefing.

Daniel and Brenda treated themselves to a nice lunch at Starlight and then drove across town, back to the station. Leila arrived a little later, went directly to Izzy's office, and asked the three of them to meet her in the conference room at 4:00 p.m.

"Let's compare notes," she said, grabbing a marker and standing at the whiteboard. "Hollenbeck arrested a guy named Sanchez for Espinoza's murder. They've got a snitch in the gang and the murder weapon was found in Sanchez's apartment. I went to the station today and they let me interview Sanchez. He claims he doesn't know the name of the guy who hired him. The guy spoke Spanish, called his cell phone, and paid in cash, delivered to a locker at Union Station. We got the cell out of Evidence and I downloaded the data and gave it to Izzy to trace. Hollenbeck found the cash in Sanchez's apartment. The lab's checking it for serial numbers and fingerprints."

Daniel grinned and gave her a thumbs-up. "Outstanding."

"It was a burner phone," Izzy said. "The only useful information I have is that it pinged on a cell tower in Houston, Texas. When I reviewed the phone bill from the modeling agency that Daniel got, I noticed they also got a call from a Houston burner phone, not the same number."

"Someone's being careful," Leila said. She turned to Daniel. "Do you know anything about that phone call?"

"Yeah. Someone was trying to trace Nicole to invite her to another fundraiser. Unfortunately, the manager didn't remember the man's name. She said she told him Nicole no longer worked for them."

"The most interesting thing about Houston is that it's the headquarters of Ace Fossil Fuels. Kenneth Palmer is their CEO. I did a deep dive into him, as requested," Izzy said.

"Do tell." Leila handed Izzy the dry erase marker and sat down.

"He's 72 years old, Texas born and bred. Went to college at Texas A&M and business school at Wharton. Family is loaded. Kenneth's the oldest son. Has a sister and younger brother. Neither of them is in the oil business. Palmer learned it from the ground up. He worked on offshore oil platforms during his college summers. He's quite a player with the ladies. He's on his fourth wife and they keep getting younger. This one is 24 and a former model. He's got three adult children and a two-year-old."

"And he still has time to go to fundraisers and rape women. What a guy!" Leila said.

"His family are big political donors and Palmer's been in Fuchs' inner circle for years. Go back in time to the gossip columns, you can see the two of them attending Miss America contests. His firm gave mega dollars to one of Fuchs' PACs."

"Hence the possibility of his being offered a cabinet position," Daniel said.

Izzy nodded.

"He have a fixer?" Brenda asked. "Somehow, I don't see a 72-year-old CEO hiring a gang member to kill a woman he raped."

"Good point," Izzy said. "I've looked at the higher level company employees. His office manager is a guy named Hector Vargas. He might speak Spanish. I'll check out anyone with a Spanish surname who might have direct contact with Palmer."

"I'm wondering how Palmer found Nicole. Could he have hired a PI firm?" Daniel asked.

"Very possible. We're going to need a lot of phone data and some grunts to check it out. It's going to be tedious, and it may lead nowhere," Izzy said.

Leila turned to Brenda. "Any luck finding other suspects?"

She shook her head. "Nicole was very well-liked at her job, had no known romantic relationship, and none of her co-workers had a motive to kill her. Quite the opposite, actually. We found lots of friends for her. Which is a good thing. She probably needs them just as much as we need suspects."

CHAPTER TWENTY

Friday, October 28th 2016

HANNAH FINISHED HER FRIDAY MORNING POST-surgical rounds and took the elevator to the rehabilitation floor. She had never been there in all the years she worked at Memorial.

Hannah inquired at the nurse's station, was directed to Nicole's room, and was pleased to see a fresh-faced young police officer seated on a chair outside the door.

"I'm Dr. Hannah Kline, Ms. Adler's obstetrician," she said, showing her ID.

"I know who you are, Dr. Kline. I've worked with your husband." He gave her a big grin. "I'm Alberto Figueroa."

"I'm happy to see Nicole's getting protection," Hannah said.

"I don't know how much longer protection will be authorized for. I hope they crack the case soon."

Hannah knocked on the door and glanced in. Nicole was sitting up in bed and smiled at her.

"I'm glad to see you, Dr. Kline. Can we talk after you check me out?"

"Of course," Hannah said. She examined the incision, made sure the uterus was firm, and assessed Nicole's bleeding, which was minimal. All vital signs were normal.

"You've pretty much recovered from your C-section. If you weren't in rehabilitation, I'd be sending you home and telling you to come see me in six weeks for a final post-op exam."

"I'm not sure I can get to your office in six weeks," Nicole said.

"I don't expect you to. I'll come see you."

"Does this mean you won't be making rounds on me every day any longer?" Nicole's face looked stricken.

"Not official medical rounds, but I promise to come up and visit and see how you're doing. Is there anything I can help you with now?"

Nicole bit her lip and hesitated. "I don't know what to do about Jeremy, Dr. Kline. It seems my priest was pressuring me to sign him over to a Catholic agency for adoption before the accident, but I never signed the paperwork, which tells me I had mixed feelings, even before he was born."

"I can tell you have mixed feelings now. What are you thinking?"

"I spoke to the rehabilitation doctor yesterday. For the first time, I have some hope of regaining function, at least in my hands and arms. I don't want to make a final decision about Jeremy until I know if I'm going to get better."

"That seems like a sensible idea to me," Hannah said. "It's never good to make major life decisions in the midst of a crisis."

"It's not that easy. The hospital can't keep him here the

whole time I'm in rehabilitation. I'd have to send him to foster care and I'm scared to death that some stranger might abuse him. You hear such horrible stories about foster care."

"Have you spoken to the social worker? I have to admit that I don't know much about the foster care system and how it works. Maybe there's some way you can vet the foster parents."

An embryonic thought was beginning to form at the back of Hannah's mind. Part of her was afraid to access it. "Nicole, let me make some calls and see what I can find out. Perhaps I can help you find a different solution for Jeremy's care. Give me a day or two."

"Would you help me? I'd be so grateful."

"I'll do whatever I can. I can't promise to find you a better solution, but I will promise to try."

Hannah waited until dinner was almost over to tell Daniel about her day. She filled three bowls with chocolate chip ice cream, spooned some fudge sauce over Zoe's, and sent her to her room to work on her homework.

She came up behind Daniel, reached over his shoulder to place his bowl in front of him, and then put her arms around him, kissing the top of his head.

He responded, taking her hands in his and kissing her palms. "Are you my dessert, or is it the chocolate chip ice cream?"

"You can have both, but in the proper order. You don't have to worry that I'll melt." She took her chair and smiled at him.

"You look as if you've had a good day, sweetheart."

"I had an okay day, but I do have a possible good thought and wanted to share it."

"I'm all ears."

Hannah took a breath. How to begin... "You know I was heartbroken when I had that miscarriage. But after a while, I tried to rationalize it by thinking maybe it was for the best. With all our responsibilities maybe we don't have the bandwidth for another child."

Daniel reached over and took her hands. "I know. Are you thinking any differently now?"

"I stopped in at the NICU yesterday and wound up feeding Nicole's baby. He's pretty adorable. Then I made rounds on Nicole this morning. She wants more time to see if she can recover enough function to keep him, instead of giving him up for adoption."

"It's hard to imagine how. She'd need a full-time staff and lots of money."

"There's more. He can't stay in the hospital for the time that Nicole will be in rehabilitation. It might take several months. They told her she might have to put him in foster care. She was very upset at the idea."

"I don't blame her. I've seen some pretty bad outcomes in the L.A. Foster Care system."

"Daniel, what if we offered to help her by fostering Jeremy ourselves? We already have a full-time housekeeper who helps care for Zoe when we're at work. If Emilia is willing, we could do it."

"Hannah, are you thinking that if Nicole can't take him back, we would adopt him?"

"I'm hoping that she'll regain enough movement to be able to care for him, and in the process of fostering, we can learn if we're willing to try again."

"Love, I've always been willing to try again, but you're

the one who has to do the hard part and be pregnant. I don't think fostering is a good idea. One of the things I love best about you is how compassionate you are, but this seems like breaching a boundary. I'm worried that you haven't thought it through."

"Too much heart, not enough head?" Maybe Daniel had a point. The impulse had been strong and spontaneous.

"What happens if you fall in love with this baby? Wouldn't it break your heart to have to part with him? What about Zoe? How would she feel if she had a baby brother for a few months and then had to give him back? Or, on the other hand, if Nicole can't keep him, are you prepared to adopt? If you aren't sure about being able to manage another child, why put us both in this difficult position?"

"Damn it. You're right. I didn't think it through."

Daniel stood up and took her in his arms. "I'm sorry, sweetheart, truly. But just know that if you want to try again, I'm on board."

"Really? I didn't know how you felt."

"I didn't want to pressure you, especially since you were grieving, and I had just brought a teenager into our lives. I saw how much you struggled to accept Josh."

It was true. She was stunned when she learned that her brand-new husband had a biological son he knew nothing about.

"In the meantime, why don't we do something else to help Nicole? There's a very smart attorney who offered her pro bono help. How about we call her in the morning?"

CHAPTER TWENTY-ONE

Monday, October 31st, 2016

DANIEL WAS AT HIS DESK, ELBOWS ON THE DESKTOP, head supported in his hands, staring at a blank computer screen.

"You look deep in thought," Brenda said, as she walked to her desk and deposited her purse in a drawer. "What's up?"

"Frustration." Maybe it would help to run it by Brenda before Leila came in this morning. "We have one suspect and no real evidence. We think Palmer raped her, but Nicole doesn't remember. We have some burner phones from Houston but no way to prove they're connected to him. There's no evidence he traced her or knew she was pregnant. All we have is a pie-in-the-sky theory."

"True. So, let's think this out. What do we need in the way of evidence to back this up?"

"First of all, proof that Palmer fathered Nicole's child. We can get DNA from the baby, but we also need DNA from Palmer. Second, we need to prove that Palmer became aware she was pregnant and felt threatened. Third, we need to prove Palmer hired Espinoza to get rid of her. Unfortunately, Espinoza may not have known who hired him, and it doesn't matter anyway, because he's dead."

"To get DNA legally, we either have to file rape charges or file for paternity support. I doubt Nicole would agree to do either," Brenda said. "Has she decided what she wants to do about the baby?"

"Not yet. Hannah and I made an appointment to talk to Samantha Copeland at lunchtime today. She's offered Nicole her pro bono services. She might have a strategy to deal with whatever social service options are available when Nicole gets out of rehabilitation."

"I've never known anyone that disabled," Brenda said. "I'd never given a thought before on how people who can't care for themselves and have no families manage."

"Me neither," said Daniel, "and it makes me feel guilty. Sometimes we have no clue about how much other people suffer unless it's in our faces. Maybe I'm hoping the best way to feel better is by doing all I can to help one person."

It was after four in the afternoon and Nicole was exhausted. The occupational therapist had spent an hour trying to teach her to send emails with her voice. As someone who'd never felt comfortable with computers, it made her head spin.

Then the physical therapist came, leaving her feeling numb and in pain.

Next came lunch, being fed hospital food by a bored aide. Using her jaw muscles to chew and trying to swallow felt like running a marathon.

After lunch, the nurse brought Jeremy for a visit, but he was fussy and cried until she begged to have him returned to the nursery. All she wanted was to sleep.

"By the way, Dr. Kline called to let you know she would be coming by about five o'clock," the nurse said, as she swaddled Jeremy. She flattened Nicole's bed, fluffed her pillows and blanket, and turned out the light, wheeling the bassinet out of the room.

When Nicole opened her eyes, Dr. Kline was seated at her bedside.

"How long have you been here?" Nicole asked.

"A few minutes. I didn't want to wake you. You looked as if you needed the sleep."

"I did, thank you."

"I brought Samantha Copeland with me. She's waiting outside at the nursing station. Detective Ross and I met with her earlier this afternoon to see what she could do to help with Jeremy. She has an interesting idea. Shall I ask her to come in?"

"Can you help me sit up first?"

Dr. Kline took the bed control and elevated the back of the bed. "I can wait in the hallway, so you two can have a private conversation."

"Please stay, Dr. Kline. I feel calmer when you're here, and I don't want to miss anything important."

"Of course." The doctor left the room and returned with Samantha Copeland. The attorney was carrying a brown leather briefcase.

"I'm glad to see you out of the ICU," Samantha said, as she pulled up a chair and seated herself beside Nicole's bed.

"I've been thinking about you a great deal, and I have an idea that might help."

"I'm all ears. At least those are working," Nicole said.

"When we met before, we talked about criminal rape charges against Kenneth Palmer. Unfortunately, your amnesia would make that a very difficult trial with no guarantee of conviction. Even with DNA evidence proving he was Jeremy's father, he would just claim consensual sex."

"I understand that. I thought that's why we already ruled that out. What I need is a way to keep Jeremy, if I can improve enough to make that possible, and to care for him in the meantime without giving him away."

"Precisely," Samantha said. "That means you need money. Lots and lots of money, and Kenneth Palmer is a billionaire oilman. He also has a very much younger wife and a two-year-old kid, and is being considered for a cabinet position if Fuchs wins the election."

"God forbid," Nicole said.

"Palmer is vulnerable. The last thing he needs is bad publicity. So, we file a civil suit for child support. We can legally get his DNA that way, and I'll bet that he and his attorneys will want to settle out of court with a non-disclosure agreement."

"So he gets away with rape and possibly being behind my murder attempt? I'm not sure I buy that idea. What if he claims we had consensual sex and tries to take Jeremy away from me?"

"At this point, Detective Ross doesn't have enough hard evidence to charge him with rape and no District Attorney would file the case. A civil suit is the only way of getting any justice for you and your son. I doubt he'd try to take Jeremy. Why rock the boat if he can make everything go away with a confidential settlement?" Samantha said.

"What do you think, Dr. Kline?"

"I'm not a lawyer, Nicole, but this suggestion makes sense to me and sounds as if it could help you accomplish your goal."

"The plan," Samantha said, "is to negotiate for enough money to purchase a home for you, and to pay for 24/7 healthcare workers to care for you and Jeremy, as well as child support. That's a drop in the bucket for him and the possibility of a productive life for you."

"I don't know. It sounds good, but what if it's not that easy?" While these were two smart women, and her gut told her she could trust them, she was still apprehensive.

"There's only one thing that concerns me," Samantha said. "When you first met with me, before the accident, you told me you had seen your rapist on television and identified him as Kenneth Palmer."

"I'll have to take your word for it. I can't remember our conversation."

"I recorded it so I would remember," Samantha said. "You told me he approached you at a fundraiser and offered to introduce you to a producer."

"I would have fallen for that. I wanted to act, not model."

"He escorted you to another room and gave you a drink. You were smart enough to ask for sparkling water, not alcohol, but after you drank it, you felt dizzy. When you awoke you were on the sofa with your dress pulled up to your waist and your panties on the floor."

"Date rape drug," Hannah said.

"Most likely," Samantha agreed. "You knew you'd been raped, but had no memory of Palmer doing it, and you chose not to report it and have a rape kit taken."

"I was probably terrified and humiliated. A good Catholic girl should have known better."

"Don't blame yourself," Hannah said. "This wasn't your fault."

"The problem is, was it just Palmer, or were you gang raped by him and some cronies while you were unconscious?" Samantha said. "If that happened, Palmer's paternity test could be negative. It would be nice to be certain."

"I have a thought," Hannah said. "Loads of people are doing ancestry DNA tests and sharing their data. We could submit Jeremy's DNA under an assumed name. Maybe we'll get a hit with one of Palmer's relatives."

"That's a brilliant idea," Samantha said. "What do you think, Nicole? It would be very helpful to know if Palmer is Jeremy's father."

"Would you wait to file the suit until the results come back?" Nicole asked.

"No. Palmer is at his most vulnerable right now. These civil suits take a good deal of time. We would probably get Jeremy's results back before Palmer complies with the order to send in a paternity sample. And we might not get any hits on our genetic profile. It's just extra data that could be useful in court."

"So, when do you plan to file?" Nicole asked.

"As soon as you give me the okay."

Nicole thought it over. "Let's do it. But what do I do to care for Jeremy while I'm in rehab and the lawsuit is in process?"

"I've thought about that as well. I want to help you, and I've come up with an idea for you to avoid foster care. If you give me your power of attorney, I'll hire a childcare provider and supervise Jeremy's care while you're unable to do so. I promise I will find you someone trustworthy. But you'll have the final say over who we hire and his care."

"How can I possibly pay for that?"

"I'll advance you the funds. My firm will earn it back when you settle this case."

Tears of gratitude welled up in Nicole's eyes. She felt like a huge weight had just been lifted off her chest. "How do I sign?"

CHAPTER TWENTY-TWO

Tuesday, November 8th, 2016

A WEEK LATER, IT WAS FINALLY ELECTION NIGHT. Hannah took the hot buttered popcorn out of the microwave and poured it into a large bowl. She removed three glasses from a cabinet, and a bottle of soda from the refrigerator, and placed them all on a tray, which she carried into the den. She had stashed a bottle of champagne in the refrigerator earlier. She intended to open it if Fuchs lost, and the country had finally elected its first woman president.

Daniel turned on CNN and Zoe poured herself a large glass of soda. The polls had just closed on the East Coast. The polls had been promising, and Fuchs was such a revolting candidate, Hannah couldn't imagine that any intelligent person would vote for him. She grabbed a handful of popcorn, stretched her feet out on the ottoman, and relaxed.

"You're invested in this election," Daniel said.

"It's the first time I've ever been politically active, other than to donate money. It's a combination of wanting to see a smart woman running things and being repelled by the opposition. Fuchs' supporters would like women to become handmaidens."

At eight o'clock, Zoe headed upstairs to bed. "You can tell me who won in the morning."

By nine o'clock, Hannah's stomach was beginning to reflect her anxiety. The numbers were closer than she had anticipated.

By ten o'clock, she couldn't watch any longer.

"He's going to win." She wanted to cry and scream at the same time.

"It's surreal," Daniel said. "I can't believe it. Not only that, but he'll appoint the head of an oil company as secretary of energy. What difference does it make if we destroy the planet as long as the oil companies make money?"

Hannah turned off the TV and the den light. She grabbed Daniel's hand and headed upstairs to the bedroom. Once there, she took off her clothes and threw them on the floor.

"I need something to help me sleep," she said, pushing him toward the bed.

Daniel didn't resist. Usually, their lovemaking was leisurely and tender. Not this time. It felt fast and desperate, as if it was the only thing that could take their minds off the disaster that was coming to Washington, DC.

"Do you think Fuchs will be that bad?" Daniel asked afterward, as she lay with her head on his shoulder.

"I think he'll be worse than you or I could possibly imagine."

CHAPTER TWENTY-THREE

Wednesday, November 9th, 2016

WHEN HANNAH ENTERED THE HOSPITAL, THE PLACE felt like a funeral home. No cheery "Good morning, Dr. Kline," or chatting in the elevator. People walked with heads down and glum expressions. None of her patients had their televisions on.

Hannah made her rounds quickly with a minimum of conversation. No one brought up the election. Her next stop was a visit to Nicole to get consent for a genetic sample on Jeremy. The kits had arrived in her office the previous week.

There was no guard at Nicole's door when she arrived. Hannah frowned, wondering if he was on a bathroom break.

Nicole was awake and with a nurse who was taking her vital signs.

"Where's your doorman?" Hannah asked.

"They discontinued him yesterday. I guess they think I'm safe now."

"Don't worry, Dr. Klein," the nurse said. "Visitors have to

check in at the lobby, and hospital security won't let anyone up to see Nicole unless she approves."

Hannah just nodded. No point in upsetting Nicole, but she was going to call Daniel about this when she got to her office.

"I've got the paperwork for Jeremy's tests," she said. "Nicole, if you give your verbal consent, your nurse can sign as a witness. Then I'll head to the nursery and get the samples this morning."

"I consent," Nicole said.

The nurse signed the form and left the room.

"I'm still in shock after last night," Nicole said.

"Me too."

"Do you think this will affect our lawsuit?"

"I think it should make him more willing to settle," Hannah said. "He can't afford to have this publicized while he's being considered for a cabinet position."

"Ms. Copeland told me he was served with papers last week," Nicole said.

"I wish I could have been a fly on the wall when he got them."

"We'll just have to be patient. Your job is to do everything possible to get stronger."

Nicole smiled. "I'm feeling very motivated to get better. I can't thank you enough. I wish I could hug you."

"I can hug you," Hannah said.

Daniel got to the station early. He needed some alone time to think about the case before his colleagues arrived and started talking politics. A fair number of police officers admired Fuchs and had no doubt voted for him. They found his aggressive masculinity appealing. There would be arguments today as the Fuchs fans gloated and the opposition fumed. Daniel usually avoided talking politics with anyone but Brenda, who shared his views.

"You're an early bird." Leila greeted him as she entered the space.

She was smiling. Was she a Fuchs fan?

"What's up?" Daniel asked.

"Got a call this morning from Calloway at Hollenbeck. We've finally got a promising lead."

"No kidding. What?"

"They got fingerprints off the cash and they were in the system. A guy named Hector Vargas. The serial numbers traced to an account for an LCC in Houston with confidential ownership."

"Doesn't Vargas work for Palmer?" Daniel asked.

"Do you have any idea how many guys named Hector Vargas live in this country?"

"Not a clue, but I'm not a believer in coincidences. Does Vargas have a record?"

"He was arrested at age nineteen for assault during a gang fight in Texas."

"Let me guess, the same gang as Espinoza and Sanchez?"

Leila grinned. "You got it. I just asked Izzy to see if Hector Vargas flew to Los Angeles from Houston recently. Maybe he was the delivery man for all that cash."

"Did the Hollenbeck team find any cash in Espinoza's apartment?"

"I don't know, but he must have been paid to run over Nicole. I'll call and get an update."

Daniel nodded and returned to his desk. Brenda was there with chocolate-covered doughnuts and coffee.

"I've already eaten three of these," she said. "I stuff my face when I'm depressed."

"You're giving the rest of them to me? Do they help the depression?"

"No, but a full stomach calms the nausea I've been feeling since last night."

Daniel squeezed her shoulder. "Hannah's go-to is ice cream. I'd better pick up a few pints before I go home tonight. We're both in a pretty vile mood. I've never seen her cry before over an election."

"Join the club. Take my mind off it. What's the turn-around on the baby's DNA testing?"

"Four to eight weeks."

"I hate waiting for results," Brenda said.

"Me too, but maybe Izzy will find something useful soon. I'm going to the break room to get some coffee to wash down your doughnut. Want some?"

Brenda shook her head. "I'm too wired already."

As Daniel entered the break room he was surprised to see Alberto Figueroa nursing a mug of black caffeine. "What are you doing at the station? I thought you were assigned to Memorial."

"I was. The chief called me back yesterday. He said he couldn't spare two guys for 24/7 coverage any longer. Too many other cases going on. Hospital security is taking over."

"I hope they're up to it. I don't think Nicole's out of danger yet." Daniel poured himself a large cup of coffee, adding sugar and milk.

"I hope you're wrong," Alberto said.

CHAPTER TWENTY-FOUR

Thursday, November 10th, 2016, 4:00 AM

NIGHTS IN THE HOSPITAL WERE ALWAYS QUIET, AND 4:00 a.m. was a particularly dead time. The nurses had all finished their 3:00 a.m. vital signs and were charting in the break room, in between coffee and what passed for lunch on the night shift. The ward clerk on the rehabilitation floor was at her desk, reading an old copy of People magazine. No one was paying attention.

The night janitor, dressed in scrubs and wearing a surgical hat on his head and a pair of latex gloves, shuffled down the corridor, pushing a cart with a large garbage can, cleaning fluid, mops, and broom. He stopped at the staff bathroom, went through the door with his bucket, mop, and cleaning fluid, and swabbed the floor. Then he walked down the corridor, picking up the occasional piece of paper or other debris from the day.

Pausing in front of a patient door, he glanced up and down the hall. Seeing no one, he turned the lever and glanced in. The patient appeared to be asleep. Silently, he entered the room.

Her arms were resting on a pillow on either side of her slim body. He slipped one pillow out from underneath her and held it over her face. He knew she wouldn't be able to fight him. He felt her trying to lift her head and grunting as he pressed harder. Finally, her head fell back and the sounds stopped. He held the pillow tightly until the motion of her chest ceased. With one gloved hand, he felt her neck for a pulse. There was nothing.

Lifting the pillow, he replaced it gently beneath her arm, in the same position as the opposite one. Checking her pulse to be sure his job was done, he left the room and continued his slow shuffle down the hall.

When he reached the utility closet, he put away his equipment and exited the unit via the staircase. Mission accomplished.

CHAPTER TWENTY-FIVE

Thursday, November 10th, 2016

HANNAH HAD A 7:30 A.M. SURGERY SCHEDULED FOR Thursday morning. On the plus side, it was the first case of the day, so there was no chance she would be late for her office. On the minus side, her partner was not a morning person and had to be well caffeinated so she could keep her eyes open in the OR. Hannah threw on a pair of scrubs and sneakers, stuck her long red hair into a ponytail, and kissed her drowsy spouse goodbye.

Arriving at the hospital parking lot, she headed to the postpartum unit to discharge a patient, and then to the rehabilitation floor for a quick check on Nicole. This visit was strictly a social call, but Hannah knew how much her presence meant to her patient and didn't want to disappoint her.

She arrived at 6:45 a.m. The night nurses were busy reporting to the day shift before 7:00 a.m. rounds. Hannah waved to the staff and headed for Nicole's room.

When Hannah entered, Nicole appeared to be asleep,

but something about her face caused Hannah a deep feeling of unease. Nicole's mouth was open, her face waxy and pale. Hannah tiptoed to the bedside. With a sense of panic, she placed her hand above Nicole's mouth and nose and felt no brush of air, noticed no chest movement. When she placed two fingers on her carotid artery, she detected no pulse. Nicole's body was cold.

Heart racing, Hannah left the room, closing the door behind her. Had Nicole died in the night and no one had noticed? Had something more sinister happened? Where the hell was her police guard? Hannah took out her phone and called the nursing station.

"This is Dr. Klein. I need the charge nurse, stat. I'm outside Nicole Adler's room."

The charge nurse appeared a moment later, power-walking toward Hannah.

"Is something wrong?" she asked, breathing heavily.

"Very wrong. Nicole Adler is dead."

"Are you sure? She seemed to be doing well."

"Of course, I'm sure."

The charge nurse turned to enter the room.

"Don't go in there. I'm going to call the detectives. Nicole was the victim of a murder attempt. I don't know if this was a natural death or if someone finished the job. Who saw her last?"

The nurse stopped and stared at Hannah, eyes wide. "I can't believe this wasn't a natural death. Let me check the computer."

There was a desk unit outside every pod of rooms. She sat down, logged in, and pulled up Nicole's chart. "She was seen at 3:15 a.m. for vital signs. They appear normal."

"Please call hospital security to guard this door and

make sure no one goes in before the detectives arrive. They will want to talk to you."

"Yes, Doctor." The charge nurse gave her a skeptical glance and walked at a normal pace back to her office.

Hannah called Daniel.

~

Daniel was at the breakfast table eating Honey Nut Cheerios with Zoe when his cell rang.

"Hi, honey, everything okay?"

Hannah was breathing heavily and her voice, when she finally spoke was shaky. "Nicole is dead."

"What?!"

"I went to her room. There was no police guard at her door and she was lying there, cold and dead. He wasn't here yesterday either, when I made rounds. Why the hell were her guards pulled?"

"I asked the same thing yesterday. I was told the chief canceled guard duty because he couldn't spare the manpower. But I was assured that hospital security was going to take over."

"Great job they did." Daniel heard a sob.

"Sweetheart, do you have any reason to think this wasn't natural? She was pretty compromised."

"Someone tried to run her over. She had just filed a civil suit against the man she thought raped her and tried to have her killed. Less then a week after he's served with papers, her protection detail disappears and suddenly she's dead. Don't you think it's worth looking into?"

Daniel took a breath, mentally calculating how long it would take him to drop Zoe off at carpool, notify Leila, and get to Memorial. "Of course, I do. I'm going to call Leila and we'll have a team get there as soon as possible. In the meantime, don't let anyone into that room. Call hospital security. We'll treat this as a crime scene until proven otherwise."

"I just did all that. Don't you think I learned anything being married to a homicide detective?" Hannah said.

"I knew I could count on you."

"I have surgery, so tell Leila to make it snappy."

CHAPTER TWENTY-SIX

Thursday, November 10th, 2016

LEILA WAS THE FIRST TO ARRIVE. HANNAH, SITTING AT the nurse's station, spotted her coming down the hall and breathed a sigh of relief.

"I'm glad to see you," Hannah said. "The hospital security guard is outside the door and no one but me has gone in since I discovered Nicole's body. The charge nurse is waiting for you. I have to go, or I'll be late for surgery."

"Did you touch anything in the room?" Leila asked. "We may need to fingerprint you."

"I touched the door handle and bent down to check Nicole's carotid pulse to confirm her death. Nothing else. I know not to mess up a possible crime scene."

"Does it look like a crime scene?" Leila asked.

"Nothing obvious, but that's for you and Daniel to judge, and the medical examiner. The nurses think I'm being paranoid."

"I hope they're right and it was a natural death, but

thanks for doing all the right things. I'll catch up with you later today. Where's Daniel?"

"On his way. Should be here soon, depending on the traffic from the Westside."

Hannah headed toward the elevators, hoping she wasn't so agitated that it would interfere with her surgical skills. She needed to keep her mind on the task at hand even though all she wanted to do was cry.

Daniel arrived to find Leila at the nursing station, waiting for him.

"Detective Ross, this is Margaret Bailey, the nurse in charge of the night shift. Hannah asked her to wait until we got here."

"Thank you for waiting, Ms. Bailey. Did anything unusual happen last night?"

Bailey shrugged her shoulders.

Leila took out a pad and pen and began taking notes.

"There were a few visitors who left at 8:30 p.m., when visiting hours ended. Otherwise, it was totally quiet."

"Did Nicole Adler have a visitor?"

"No. Dr. Kline is the only person who sees her regularly, other than the rehabilitation staff."

"Who saw her alive last?"

"Her nurse took her vitals at 3:15 a.m." Bailey sounded annoyed, as though a patient's death was much ado about nothing.

"I'd like a list of everyone on the rehabilitation night shift, please," Daniel said. "What time does the night shift start?"

"Eleven p.m."

"Is everyone who was on last night also scheduled for tonight?" Daniel asked.

Bailey nodded.

"Good. We'll be back to interview them tonight," Leila said.

Daniel took a breath. "That will be all for now. We'll give you a written statement to review and sign if there turns out to be anything suspicious about this death."

He and Leila walked to Nicole's room. The hospital security guard was sitting on a chair outside the door.

"I'm Detective Ross. This is Detective Abebe. We're going inside now. Don't allow any hospital employees into the room. Our forensic team should arrive any minute." Daniel and Leila put on their gloves and shoe covers and entered Nicole's room. Nicole's body was under the covers, arms resting on pillows. Daniel approached, pulled back the covers, and examined her neck.

"No bruising or signs of strangulation. She doesn't have an IV any longer, so if someone wanted to give her a toxic substance, they would have had to inject it. We'll leave it to the medical examiner to run a toxicology screen and look for signs of injection."

"She would have been helpless to fight anyone," Leila said.

"If she was sleeping, she could have been murdered before she even woke up," Daniel agreed.

Nicole's lids were closed and he held them open with one hand, examining her eyes with a small flashlight.

"Look at the capillaries," he said. "This is a sign of being smothered. Let's check out the pillows."

Leila removed the pillow under Nicole's left arm. The linens were crisp all the way around.

Daniel removed the right-sided one. The underside was

creased and slightly damp. "Look at this. I'll bet it's her saliva. We need forensics to test this. It looks like someone snuck in here and held a pillow over her face long enough to kill her."

"Fucking hospital security. This wouldn't have happened if someone was guarding her door." Leila's face was contorted in fury.

"I know. But sometimes, even your best efforts can't prevent a determined killer." Daniel replaced the pillow and turned away "Let's get out of here and brief the forensic team. We need to find out if there are any security cameras on this floor and get the footage. I'm going to notify Samantha Copeland to come here and take custody of Jeremy. For all we know, he might be the next target. Someone is going to great lengths to protect himself."

CHAPTER TWENTY-SEVEN

Thursday, November 10th, 2016

Back at the station, Daniel was pulled into meetings. When Leila came in later that afternoon, he waved her over to his desk. "I just met with the chief. Since this is now a homicide investigation, he's asked me to take the lead."

"The chief's the boss," Leila said. Her face was expressionless.

Daniel couldn't tell if she was annoyed or disappointed. He continued, trying to be as tactful as possible. "I told him I wanted you to partner on the case. You've been doing a great job and you're familiar with all the evidence. He agreed."

Leila nodded. Daniel called a team meeting and quickly briefed Brenda and Izzy. Then he turned to Leila. "Leila, did you get any footage?"

"I did. They have cameras at the elevators, the stairwell, and in the hallway. Sometimes rehabilitation patients like to take walks on their own, but they aren't supposed to walk without staff. The hospital has cameras to make sure no one falls and sues. Take a look."

Daniel held out his hand for the flash drive and plugged it into his computer. "Let's start with the hallway at 3:15 that morning."

They saw a nurse leave Nicole's room at 3:20 a.m. and walk into the adjacent one. Another nurse was taking vital signs on the opposite side of the hallway. By 3:30 a.m., both of them had walked back to the nurse's station. The hall was empty for the next half hour. Then, Daniel spotted the janitor. He was wearing a surgical cap, gloves and scrubs, and his back faced the camera. They saw him enter the bathroom, come out, and mop the hallway floor. A few minutes later, he paused at the entrance of Nicole's room.

He glanced up and down the hall, and for a second there was a view of his face. Then he entered the room. Daniel noted the time.

Six minutes later, the janitor left, strolled down the hall, put his equipment in the closet, and exited by the back stairs.

"Wait," Leila said. "There's more. The obstetrical floor has cameras in the stairway, just in case someone absconds with a baby that isn't theirs."

A moment later, the janitor was seen descending the stairs. The camera caught him exiting on the mezzanine level where the employee parking was located. The video paused and then caught him driving out of the lot in a black Ford Focus.

"Did you get the license plate?" Daniel asked.

Leila rolled her eyes. "I checked it on the way over. It belongs to a Budget Rental near the airport. Rented on Wednesday by a Jesus Zepata."

"Sounds like an alias to me," Brenda said.

"Izzy, do you think you can run some facial recognition on the glimpse we had of the guy's face?"

Izzy nodded. "I can, but unless he has a social media presence or a record, I might not get a hit."

"I'm hoping it might be Hector Vargas," Daniel said.

"You asked me to check if Hector Vargas was in Los Angeles near the time of the murder attempt. He flew from Houston to L.A. on October 20th, and took a red-eye back on the 22nd, just in time to pay for the attempted murder. He also flew to L.A. yesterday, and is currently on a plane back to Texas."

"Suspicious but hardly conclusive," Brenda commented. "We don't have enough hard evidence to arrest him. Isn't it more likely he hired someone to do the job?"

"Maybe, but it's worth checking. Leila, get that car impounded and over to forensics. We should be able to get some fingerprints. Izzy, can you find Vargas's driver's license photo or something on Facebook?" Daniel asked.

"I'll do my best," Izzy said. "I can run through some of the social media accounts on what's left of today, but I'm going to be out of town for the Veteran's Day weekend. If I don't get a hit quickly, I won't have anything for you before Monday afternoon."

"Speaking of holidays," Leila said, "have you spoken to Samantha Copeland about taking Jeremy into custody this weekend? The sooner the better."

"I have. She's getting together all the paperwork and lining up someone to take care of him. She's hoping to have him out of there by Monday, at the latest. In the meantime, hospital security will have someone in the nursery 24/7," Daniel said. "She's been putting plans in motion for a private, closed adoption, out of state, for his safety."

"Poor kid," Brenda said. "I just hope she finds him loving parents."

CHAPTER TWENTY-EIGHT

Saturday, November 12, 2016

THE WEEKEND SHOULD HAVE BEEN RELAXING. BOTH Hannah and Daniel were off call, but Hannah found herself agitated and on the constant verge of frustrated, angry tears. Her patient was dead, very likely murdered thanks to incompetent security, an infant was orphaned, the police seemed stymied, and there didn't seem to be a damn thing she could do about it. She ought to be spending time this weekend doing something fun with Zoe and Daniel, as a family, but she was too emotionally depleted to come up with a useful idea. She'd slept poorly Friday night, and by 5:00 a.m., she had given up trying. She sat in the kitchen, nursing a cup of coffee, and reading the Los Angeles Times online.

"Hannah, what's going on?" Daniel stood in the doorway in his pajamas, his dark hair with its recent streak of gray tousled from sleep, eyes half closed.

"You're up early," Hannah said, forcing a smile.

"I rolled over and you weren't there, so I came looking for you. Trouble sleeping?"

She nodded. "You too?"

He came over and began kneading the tension out of her shoulders. "We're probably having similar nightmares. It's been a lousy week. We're working on other cases, but this one is haunting me."

She reached up and squeezed his hand. "Any progress?"

"It's a holiday weekend. I don't expect results on anything until later in the week."

"I feel so sad for Nicole, for her son who will never know her, and so angry at whoever is responsible. I want him punished. Do you think you'll ever get enough evidence to identify and nail him?"

Daniel sat down, shaking his head. "I don't know. Everything is circumstantial."

"One of the things I've been thinking about is if we should reconsider fostering and eventually adopting Jeremy. I couldn't help Nicole while she was alive. But maybe we can do this for her."

Daniel leaned over and took her hands in his. "Sweetheart, it's too dangerous, for Jeremy and for our family. Someone ruthless wanted Nicole and her inconvenient pregnancy out of the way. You were one of her doctors. It would be too easy to trace him to you. Samantha Copeland is planning to arrange a closed adoption with a family who has no connection, personal or geographical, to Nicole. It's the best way to keep him safe."

Hannah got up and walked to the refrigerator so Daniel wouldn't see her eyes fill. Just because he was right, didn't prevent her from feeling disappointed.

"Would you like breakfast? I could scramble some eggs and cheddar."

"Sure, I'll put up a couple of slices of toast," he said.

Hannah wiped her eyes, pasted some calm on her face, and took the eggs, butter and cheese out. "You know what I think?"

"Not a clue."

"I think we need to put all this on the back burner for the weekend and take Zoe somewhere. I think she could use some parental attention."

CHAPTER TWENTY-NINE

Thursday, November 17th, 2016

Brenda was at her desk when Daniel arrived at the station Thursday morning. She turned and smiled at him as he sat down.

"The coroner just sent over the autopsy report on Nicole. We had it right. They concluded she was suffocated based on the hemorrhages in her eyes and the lung tissue, as well as the traces of her saliva on the underside of her pillow. A homicide."

"No surprise. Anything back yet on the car or the janitor's equipment?"

"Sorry. Not yet."

"I'm wondering how they knew Nicole was in Los Angeles. Do you suppose Palmer hired someone to trace her after the agency said she didn't work for them anymore?" Daniel asked.

Brenda shook her head. "Why would he? There's no shortage of attractive blonde models for fundraiser candy. There's something about this that doesn't make sense. He called the agency three months later. Nicole hadn't filed rape charges and had disappeared. Why go to the trouble to trace her or get rid of her?"

"Maybe the stakes were higher," Daniel suggested. "If he was expecting a cabinet nomination at that point, he might have wanted to be sure she wouldn't come out of the woodwork and accuse him of rape. He wouldn't be the first politician who was undone by a scandal."

"But murder? Most politicians would opt for a large financial bribe and a nondisclosure agreement. There's some other factor we're missing and until we figure it out, we aren't going to solve this case."

CHAPTER THIRTY

Sunday, December 11th 2016

A T A STARBUCKS IN SANTA MONICA, HANNAH TOOK her large vanilla latte and her laptop to a table and signed into their wi-fi. She wanted to check the email account she'd established for Jeremy, but she didn't want any of her IP addresses to be connected to it. So she needed to be sure she never accessed it from her home or office.

She'd set up the account under the name Michael Johnson, with an address at a convenience mailbox in San Diego. Michael had given permission to share his DNA profile with others looking for relatives. Hannah took a large swig of her coffee and logged in.

Jeremy's ancestry (except for a few Neanderthal genes) was entirely Western European. Half of it was British and Irish. The other half was German, with a trace of Italian. She scrolled down to the section that connected the profile with possible relatives who'd also submitted samples to the database.

There was a list of names that meant nothing to her, until one caused her jaw to drop. Oh, my God! Everything was about to get so much more complicated.

CHAPTER THIRTY-ONE

Monday, December 12, 2016

DANIEL ARRIVED LATE AT THE STATION. HE'D SPENT much of the morning at home, doing a secure search on all the names Hannah had given him from the DNA database. The conclusion was so explosive that he couldn't share it with his team. He trusted himself and Hannah with the information, but the two of them decided that the only other person who needed to know was Samantha Copeland. They had called her earlier this morning and arranged to see her after Hannah's office hours.

Leila waved at him from across the room. She was smiling. Daniel experienced a flush of guilt. He'd tried hard to gain her trust and respect and now, after all her hard work, he was concealing critical information. He walked toward her.

"Forensics are finally back," she said. "Hector Vargas's fingerprints were on the rental car but not on any of the janitor's equipment. We know he was wearing gloves. Do you think this is enough to bring him in?"

"If he were anywhere in California, I'd bring him in and question him. Unfortunately, he's in Texas. And given who employs him, we'd have a fight on our hands to extradite him to Los Angeles. The Texas attorney general would not be sympathetic," Daniel said.

"So what do we do? Let him get away with murder?"

"His defense attorney would argue that all we know is that he was in her room for six minutes and she could have been dead already. We didn't film him smothering her. The links are all circumstantial. We don't have a viable criminal case."

"Damn."

"Vargas may have been the hand that dealt the blow, but you and I both suspect he wasn't the brain with the motive behind this. We can't do anything unless we have a much stronger case, and we don't."

"So Palmer will get away with rape and murder for hire. Useful being a rich, powerful, politically connected white guy! I'm so pissed," Leila said.

"I couldn't agree with you more. I'm not giving up yet, but we have to tread carefully and keep this information under wraps, except for our team."

"What about the DNA Hannah sent out? When will it be back?"

"No luck. She got it back over the weekend. No link to any relatives connected to Palmer."

Leila made a face and turned back to her computer. Daniel walked to his desk. He hated lying to Leila. He hadn't even told her about his appointment with Samantha. She would want to accompany him and he couldn't allow that. What a horrific mess this case was turning out to be.

～

It was already dark and chilly when Hannah parked her car on Wilshire Boulevard, close to Samantha's law offices. She zipped up her lightweight down jacket and stepped onto the empty sidewalk. Shivering slightly, she hurried to the entrance of the building. A security guard signed her in, checked her purse, and pointed her toward the correct elevator. Daniel's name was already on the sign-in sheet. He was waiting for her in the corridor.

"Have you told her?" she asked.

He shook his head. "I was waiting for you."

She could see the stress in every line of his body and in the ravaged expression on his face.

"Sweetheart, you look awful. Has something else happened?"

Daniel drew her to a more private corner. "I'm struggling with this. I had to lie to my team this morning to keep it a secret. It's the kind of information that could get me fired if I conceal it from the department. The decision on how to proceed is way above my pay grade, probably at the level of California's Attorney General or the LAPD Chief of Police."

"It makes me wish we'd never sent that sample," Hannah said.

"Too late for that now," Daniel said. "Let's break the news to Samantha and see what she suggests."

The door to the law offices was locked. Hannah texted Samantha and she opened the door, leading them back to her office. Samantha looked worn out. Her grey hair was tousled and there were creases in her white silk blouse.

"Have a seat," she said, motioning them to the sofa as she lowered herself into a nearby armchair.

"Thank you for staying late to meet with us," Daniel said. "Is this room secure?"

Samantha gave him a puzzled look. "Secure, as in not bugged?"

Daniel nodded. "The information we have can't leave this room."

"I'm pretty sure it's safe, but feel free to check," she said.

Daniel took her at her word, looking beneath desks and tables, unscrewing light bulbs, and examining her landline phone.

"Let's all turn our cell phones off," he said.

Samantha complied, rolling her eyes. "If you'd told me you were so paranoid, I'd have ordered a Faraday cage from Amazon."

Hannah repressed a laugh.

"I think we're okay," Daniel said. "Hannah, please tell Samantha what you discovered yesterday."

"One set of DNA data came back," Hannah said. "Kenneth Palmer isn't Jeremy's father. It's Fuchs."

CHAPTER THIRTY-TWO

Monday, December 12th, 2016

S AMANTHA'S EYES WIDENED. "ARE YOU SURE?"

"The DNA connected him to five relatives. One was a half-brother named Adam Fuchs. The rest were distant cousins. Daniel investigated all of them."

"So Palmer didn't rape Nicole. He procured her for his buddy?"

"We don't know that," Daniel said. "Both of them could have raped her and Fuchs' sperm were faster swimmers. No one took a vaginal swab at the time."

"So what the hell are we supposed to do with this bomb?" Samantha got up and began pacing up and down her office floor. "No wonder an attempt was made to kill Nicole while she was still pregnant."

"The evidence won't be admissible in court. The collection was done with permission, but Hannah submitted it under a false name, from a public IP address," Daniel said. "There's no way we can accuse the incoming President of rape and expect to get a legal DNA sample. On the other hand, if this information leaks, I could lose my job, or go to jail for concealing vital evidence."

"What's happening with the civil suit?" Hannah asked. "Have you heard back from Palmer's attorney?"

"Not yet, which is interesting. If Palmer didn't rape her and knows he couldn't be Jeremy's father, why wouldn't he declare his innocence and give us a DNA sample immediately to prove it? This suggests he doesn't know which of the two of them fathered Nicole's child."

"I wonder if Fuchs knows she was pregnant, and is now dead," Hannah said. "Is he behind everything that happened to Nicole, or did Palmer orchestrate the murder to protect both of them?"

"I wish I knew the answer to that one," Samantha said. "I have no idea how to proceed from here."

"Damn. I was hoping you would," Daniel said. "I don't either. I just know I can't lie about it forever. At a minimum, I have to tell the station chief."

"Let's look at it from the perspective of our primary goal, protecting Jeremy. I think the worst possible outcome would be if he wound up in the custody of the Fuchs' family," Hannah said.

Daniel shook his head. "No, the worst outcome would be if Palmer's goons traced and killed him. Our number one priority has to be Jeremy's safety." He turned to Samantha. "How are you planning to protect him?"

"I'm still working on it," Samantha said. "I have a trusted colleague in New York looking for a family to adopt him. We can change his name and make sure he's living somewhere untraceable."

"Is that even possible these days?" Hannah asked.

"It's not easy, but I have some ideas."

"How are you going to avoid all the red tape associated with adoption?" Daniel asked.

"Better you don't know. Just leave it to me to make sure Jeremy is safe."

"Speaking of safety, the only person Palmer has to worry about right now is you. Would it be wiser to drop the lawsuit? I don't want you to be the next victim," Daniel said.

"Not yet," Samantha said. "I want to see what his next move is going to be. Now that Nicole is dead, there's less urgency about a large financial settlement. I can make sure Jeremy is given to parents who are financially secure and can support him." She returned to her chair, holding her head in her hands. "It just enrages me to see Palmer get away with this."

Hannah got up and put a hand on Samantha's shoulder. "We feel the same. Daniel and I are both devastated about Nicole's death."

Samantha turned to Daniel. "Do something, Detective. I need to see this murder solved and someone put in jail for it."

"We're doing our best, Samantha. I promise to keep you posted. But we can't talk about this on the phone or in email. It's not safe. If any of us has new information, we need to meet in person."

"I know you don't want to keep your chief out of the loop, but can we all agree to keep our mouths shut until Jeremy is safe?" Samantha said.

Daniel nodded. "But work as fast as you can, before things get out of control."

CHAPTER THIRTY-THREE

Tuesday, December 20th 2016

A WEEK LATER, THE NEXT BREAK IN THE CASE occurred courtesy of Izzy, the department's computer guru.

"Guess who's coming to town for the holidays?" Izzy announced to the team.

"Our President-elect, doing a victory dance?" Leila said.

"Right. He's holding a rally in Anaheim on Friday, followed by a dinner with mega-donors at a mansion at Dana Point. Not only that, but his lackey and candidate for energy secretary is coming with him, along with Hector Vargas."

"No kidding," Brenda said. "How'd you find that out?"

"I've been following them all on social media. When I found out about the rally, I checked airline flights to John Wayne Airport. Palmer and Vargas are flying in on Friday for the rally and dinner, and flying back on Saturday."

"Just in time for Christmas day and PR photos with the incoming first family. Strong work," Daniel said. "I don't suppose you know what hotel they've chosen?"

"Palmer and Vargas are staying at the Ritz in Dana Point. Fuchs, luckily for us, is the guest of the mega-donor hosting the dinner, so all the FBI agents will be there."

"Will there be extra security at the hotel?" Daniel asked.

"I don't know. Dana Point is covered by the Orange County Sheriff's Department. I thought it would be best if our chief contacted their chief of police and asked for cooperation in arresting our murder suspect."

"Our best bet would be to arrest him just after he checks in. We'll need some plainclothes watching the entrance of the hotel, and a few more stationed in the lobby who can follow him to his room. I'll go talk to the chief," Daniel said.

Daniel's stomach did flip-flops as he made his way to the chief's office. He was dreading this conversation. He'd rehearsed it in his car as he drove in this morning, weighing how much to share and what could reasonably be withheld.

Chief Gabriel Tucker was a large black man in his sixties, with a shiny bald head and an impressive mustache. The West L.A. Station would probably be his last posting as he was approaching retirement age. Daniel liked and respected him because he played by the book and could be counted on to be fair. That didn't mean, however, that he would let Daniel get away unscathed if he broke the rules.

"Sir, there are some major updates in the Adler homicide. Do you have time for me to brief you?"

Tucker closed the file on his desk. "Let's hear it."

"We used security footage, facial recognition, and fingerprints found in a rental car to identify a man named Hector Vargas. Vargas works for Kenneth Palmer."

"That name sounds familiar," Tucker said. "Who is he?"

"CEO of a big oil company. He's also on the shortlist for Energy Secretary in Fuchs' upcoming cabinet."

"Shit."

"Exactly, sir. We believe Nicole Adler was murdered because Palmer raped her at a Fuchs fundraiser and she became pregnant. The hit-and-run was the first attempt to kill her, but it failed. Before that happened, she met with an attorney, Samantha Copeland, and described everything she remembered about Palmer and the rape."

"Is this Vargas responsible for the hit and run?" Tucker asked.

"Not directly, but his fingerprints were on the cash that paid the driver and he was in Los Angeles at the time. The driver was killed execution-style before he could be brought in."

"Do you have enough evidence to charge Palmer with rape?"

Daniel shook his head. "No prosecutor would touch it. For such a high profile accusation the evidence would have to be airtight."

"Quite the clusterfuck." Tucker ran his hands over his bald scalp. "So, what now?"

"Palmer and Vargas will be arriving at John Wayne Airport in Orange County and staying at the Ritz in Dana Point. The President-Elect is flying in to do a victory celebration. We thought we'd arrest Vargas at the hotel. We'd appreciate it if you gave the Orange County Sheriff's Department the heads up. We have plenty of officers available for this, so we won't need them to get involved, especially since Fuchs is popular beyond the orange curtain."

"I'll make the call."

"Does this arrest need to be discussed at any higher level, sir?"

Tucker gave the question some thought, pursing his lips and tapping his fingers on the edge of his desk. "I don't think so. If we were arresting a crony of the President, I might have to mention it to the big chief, but I think we can do this as a routine arrest. Is there anything else you need to tell me?"

Was there? Should he share the bombshell from Jeremy's DNA? Samantha had been responsible for deciding to send it. Hannah wasn't a member of the LAPD and had no obligation to share information. One could argue that the DNA result was protected by attorney-client privilege.

"Not at the moment, sir. But I'll keep you updated."

Tucker nodded and picked up the file on his desk. Daniel left the office.

CHAPTER THIRTY-FOUR

Friday, December 23, 2016

THE SCHEDULE FOR THE DAY WAS SITTING ON Hannah's desk when she arrived at her office. The first new patient was Samantha Copeland. Was this a genuine medical consult or a clever way to pass on information? Either way, a medical record would be necessary, so Hannah began a new one on her iPad.

"Dr. Kline, this is Ms. Copeland," her nurse said, ushering Samantha into Hannah's consult room. Hannah rose and shook hands, murmuring a greeting as her nurse exited the room and closed the door.

"I wasn't expecting a visit from you," Hannah said.

"I'm way overdue for a mammogram and a pap smear," Samantha said, smiling. "And I figured I'd brief you at the same time. You can tell that nice husband of yours."

"Is there news?"

"Jeremy is safe. I handed him over to my colleague last weekend. The family she found was relocating due to a job transfer. There is no way anyone in their new neighborhood would know that Jeremy is adopted. I kept no records. I don't know the identity or location of his new family. The adoption was handled privately in New York and the records are sealed. I've done everything I could to make sure no one can track him."

Hannah exhaled. "I'm so glad. Thank you for everything. What about the lawsuit?"

"Palmer's attorney is going to be in town today. He wants to meet with me later this afternoon. I'll see what he has to say and then decide how to proceed."

"With Nicole dead and the need to keep Jeremy's whereabouts a secret, what would you do with the money if they agree to settle? Money can be traced."

"I know. I won't make any decision until I've discussed it with Detective Ross. Is he making any progress on Nicole's murder?"

"Something big is happening this afternoon. All I know is that Vargas is in L.A. and he's going to be arrested. Daniel didn't tell me the details, just that I shouldn't expect him home for dinner," Hannah said.

"That's great news, even if it's an annoying way to start a holiday weekend," Samantha said. "Our office is closing early today and I'll be done after I meet with Palmer's attorney. Why don't you come over when you're finished and we can celebrate Jeremy's safety and Vargas's arrest with a drink?"

Hannah grinned. "Sounds great. You do know I'm going to ask you about your negotiations."

"Ask away. If I've had enough to drink, I might tell you. Now, we should probably change the subject to my hot flashes. Menopause is a bitch."

◇

Daniel and Leila were seated in a Mercedes, parked close to the entrance of the Ritz. Plainclothes LAPD cops were at every hotel exit, and in the lobby, eying the elevator. The flight from Dallas had landed half an hour ago at John Wayne Airport, and they were expecting Palmer's limousine any moment.

"I think they're here," Leila said, as two large black limos pulled up in front of the hotel.

Bellmen surrounded the cars, opening doors and removing luggage from the trunk. Three well-dressed women and one exceptionally tall man, with the wide shoulders and demeanor of a security guard, stepped out of the first car and waited respectfully for the second one to pull up. A bellman opened the back door and Kenneth Palmer, immaculately dressed in a blue suit with a red tie, stepped out. He walked up the stairs, followed by his guard and the three staff women. The car pulled away.

"Where the hell is Vargas?" Daniel said. "He was on the flight. Why isn't he here?"

"Shit," Leila said. "We should have had someone at the airport. Do we wait for him to show up, or do we head to John Wayne and review security footage?"

"You already know the answer to that," Daniel said. He started the car.

As he headed for the freeway going north, Leila pulled up Google Maps on her phone. "Daniel, I think we should send someone else to the airport to check the footage."

"Why?"

"Vargas is Palmer's hitman. If he isn't at the hotel, where is he most likely to be going? Who is the biggest threat to his boss?"

"Samantha Copeland."

"Exactly. I think we should call and warn her, and high tail it to her office, just in case."

"You're right. You call Samantha. I'll drive. Then phone the station. Tell Brenda we need backup at Samantha's office. She can get there faster than we can."

Daniel turned on the police siren and pressed hard on the accelerator.

CHAPTER THIRTY-FIVE

BY THREE IN THE AFTERNOON, HANNAH WAS DONE with her last patient and was wishing her staff happy holidays. The office was festive and loaded with gifts from colleagues and patients: baskets of fattening holiday goodies, flower arrangements, good wines, and a few best-sellers from patients who knew her taste in reading.

She shared the goodies with her staff, selected a bottle of expensive Pinot Noir to give Samantha, and took a novel with her, in case Samantha was still occupied when she arrived.

Holiday traffic was a bear. Everyone was leaving their offices early to celebrate Christmas, or heading out to start a week-long vacation skiing or basking in the tropical sun. What should have been a fifteen-minute drive to Samantha's mid-Wilshire office building took twice as long.

Hannah pulled into the parking lot, which was almost empty, and took the elevator to the lobby, where a bored security guard asked her to sign in. The door to Copeland and Associates was unlocked and she entered.

A young and very attractive receptionist sat at a large

front desk. The central office space, visible through a glass wall behind her, was quiet and empty. The receptionist gave her a practiced smile.

"Can I help you?"

"I'm Dr. Hannah Kline. Ms. Copeland and I are going out for a drink when she finishes up today."

The receptionist's face fell. "Oh, I was expecting a lawyer who had a three o'clock appointment with her." She looked at her watch. "He's very late."

"Probably not his fault. The holiday traffic is awful."

Just then Samantha came out of her office. "Hannah, I'm so sorry. I thought I'd be done by now. Poor Jennifer wants to go home and I want a cocktail."

Hannah laughed. "Look, I've got a good book. Why don't you let Jennifer go home, and I'll sit here and pretend to be your receptionist until your appointment arrives. Then I'll read until he leaves. No hurry."

The receptionist looked hopeful.

Samantha nodded. "Go home and have a great holiday."

Jennifer grabbed her coat and left, locking the door behind her.

"This is for you, by the way," Hannah handed Samantha the wine. "Have you decided how to handle Palmer's attorney?"

"I've been thinking about strategy. We know that Palmer knows that Nicole was murdered, but we can't prove he had anything to do with it. He may think he has nothing to fear from a dead woman, but his attorney knows I could still file a lawsuit on behalf of Nicole's estate and make sure the media hears about it. I'm sure he's told Palmer to keep quiet about any interactions he had with Nicole, or if he knows whether she's alive or dead. It all goes to plausible deniability. When I spoke with him, the guy wouldn't even admit if his client knew Nicole was dead. On the other hand, Palmer may be willing to pay a substantial amount for an out-of-court confidential settlement agreement to make it all go away."

"If they offer a financial settlement, you could set up a trust for Jeremy, to be turned over to him when he turns eighteen. Surely, by then, both Palmer and Fuchs would be either deceased or out of the public eye," Hannah suggested.

"Men in power don't think like that. They think they'll be in the public eye forever."

There was a loud knock at the front door.

"Better get back to your office," Hannah whispered. "I'll bring him in."

Hannah opened the door for a man in a well-fitted gray suit and a striped blue and gray tie. His face was Hispanic, with a dark buzz cut and Frida Kahlo eyebrows framing a thick nose and puffy cheeks. Several heavy gold rings, under which she could just make out the traces of blue tattoos, adorned his hands. There was something about him that didn't look like a lawyer.

"Michael Rodriguez, Mr. Palmer's attorney," he said.

"Ms. Copeland is expecting you," Hannah said. "Follow me."

Hannah escorted him to Samantha's office. Samantha shook hands and motioned him to a seat. When she closed her door, she deliberately left it open a crack. Was she inviting Hannah to listen in? Hannah decided she was.

Samantha's phone rang.

"Do you need to take that?" Rodriguez asked.

"I'll call back later."

Rodriguez opened his briefcase and took out a file.

"Ms. Copeland. My client, Mr. Palmer, denies all your allegations. He doesn't know this woman, certainly did not rape her and is not the father of her child. This is extortion. You need to drop this threat of a lawsuit or he will be filing a complaint with the California Bar."

"Is your client prepared to defend himself in court? I imagine this would be an awkward time for him to be involved in a lawsuit, and I don't respond well to threats."

"What would it take for you to drop this case?"

"A financial settlement adequate to support this child through his college education. We both know that Mr. Palmer can well afford a settlement."

"Would your client sign an NDA?"

"An NDA is on the table if the settlement is adequate."

"Define adequate."

Samantha took a pad of paper from her desk drawer and wrote down a figure. She passed it to him.

"I'll need to discuss this with my client. May I have some privacy?"

"You can call from the waiting room. I gave my receptionist the rest of the day off."

That was a signal to Hannah to make herself scarce. She slipped into an adjoining office.

"Try her again," Daniel said.

"I've tried three times. She's not picking up. Brenda is on her way with two police cars, but she says the traffic is terrible."

"Keep trying."

Just then, Leila's phone rang. She put it on speaker.

"Ms. Copeland. Thank goodness you called back. Detective Ross and I are on our way to your office. Hector Vargas didn't go to the hotel. We are concerned he might come looking for you. Where are you now?"

"I'm meeting with Palmer's attorney at my office. He just left the room to call his boss. What does this Vargas look like?"

"Hang on. I'll text you his driver's license photo."

Texting took only a minute.

"Oh, shit. Vargas is pretending to be Palmer's lawyer and he's here. Tell Detective Ross that his wife is here too. She and I were going to go out for a drink."

Daniel's face blanched. "Samantha, I have two LAPD cars on their way to you and I'm on the 405 with my siren on, heading north as fast as I can drive. We'll be hitting the 10 freeway in minutes. Is Hannah with you now?"

"No, she's somewhere in the suite. I don't know where."

"Lock your office door. I'll call Hannah and tell her to hide."

"Too late," Samantha whispered.

The walls were too well insulated for Hannah to hear anything, so she opened her door a crack. She saw Rodriguez returning to Samantha's office after his phone call. As soon as he'd entered the room, not bothering to close the door, Hannah slipped into the hallway and crept close enough to hear.

"I'm sorry, did I interrupt you?" he said.

"Not at all. Just a friend I'm meeting for drinks later."

"My boss wants to talk to you in person. He's at the Ritz in Dana Point."

"I can make it tomorrow morning," Samantha said.

"Now," Rodriguez said. "He's busy tomorrow and he

won't take no for an answer. You want a settlement. You need to come with me."

"I'll take my own car if you don't mind. Dana Point is a long drive from here."

"He'll send you home in a limo."

"Really, Mr. Rodriguez, I prefer to drive myself. You go ahead and I'll leave as soon as I return a few phone calls."

Just then Hannah's phone vibrated with a text from Daniel's phone:

URGENT. HIDE AND LOCK YOURSELF IN.
VARGAS IS WITH SAMANTHA. LAPD ON
THE WAY.

CHAPTER THIRTY-SIX

H ANNAH TEXTED BACK:

OK.

Daniel sounded frantic. But if he thought she was going to cower like a whipped puppy in a locked room, while Samantha was in danger, he was delusional. She tiptoed back to the adjacent office and scanned it for a weapon. The only possibility appeared to be a pair of heavy bronze bookends, flanking a leather-bound set of matching law books.

She picked up one of the bookends and peeked out the door.

"Move, bitch," Vargas's voice said. "And keep your hands above your head."

Samantha appeared in the hallway, arms up, hands trembling. Vargas was behind her, holding a revolver.

"You aren't taking me to Palmer, are you?" Samantha said.

"Palmer doesn't want to see you, ever. So, I'm going to

make sure you disappear. I'd shoot you here, but then I'd get blood over your nice carpet. You're going to become a missing person."

Hannah bit her lip. She had to do something. What if he shot Samantha? What if he shot both of them? Her stomach was cramping and her hands were shaking. If they left the office, it would be too late. She took a breath, gripped the bookend, and as soon as they passed her, she opened the door.

With all the strength in her body, she brought the bookend down on his head. As he stumbled forward, she kicked him hard, in the back of the knees. He collapsed to the ground, the gun falling out of his hand.

Samantha whirled around, grabbed the gun, and pointed it at his head. "Move and I'll shoot."

He lay still on the ground, blood oozing from the laceration on his scalp.

"Oh my God," Hannah said. "Did I kill him?"

"I hope so. You saved my ass. Who knew you were such a ninja?"

"I'm not. I just took a few self-defense classes because Daniel insisted. I've been in some tight spots before. Hang on to that gun. I'm going to examine him."

Hannah knelt and checked his carotid pulse. It was beating. She moaned with relief. She'd never killed anyone and didn't want to start now.

"Call 911 and get an ambulance," Hannah said.

Samantha reached for her phone. Just then, the front door opened and four armed LAPD officers burst through, with Brenda leading the pack.

"Drop the gun!" a male voice demanded.

Samantha placed it on a desk and backed away.

"Hannah! Are you all right?" Brenda asked.

"We're both fine, but Vargas isn't. He was kidnapping Samantha at gunpoint, so I hit him on the head with a book-end. He's alive but unconscious. We need an ambulance."

Brenda holstered her gun and reached for her hand-cuffs. "Just in case he regains consciousness prematurely."

She cuffed Vargas's hands behind his back and motioned to one of the officers to help check him for weapons and turn him over.

"Someone call Detective Ross. Let him know we have Vargas, and Hannah and Ms. Copeland are safe. He doesn't need to drive a hundred miles an hour to get here."

Hannah took a deep breath. "What are we going to tell Daniel? He is going to be so pissed at me."

CHAPTER THIRTY-SEVEN

D ANIEL DROVE HIS CAR INTO THE UNDERGROUND LOT in Samantha's building and parked next to Hannah's car. There was an ambulance close to the elevator.

"That better not be here for Hannah," he said to Leila, his face grim.

"Calm down. Brenda said they were okay. You're practically vibrating in place."

Daniel pressed the elevator button and paced until it arrived. As the doors opened, two EMTs, pushing a gurney, came out. Vargas was on the gurney, cuffed, unconscious, and attended by a cop. Daniel flashed his ID.

"Everything okay in there?" he asked.

"Yes, sir. Detective Jordan is expecting you."

When Daniel reached the law office, Brenda, Hannah, and Samantha, along with two other cops, were in the waiting room. Hannah looked disheveled, but she was smiling. Daniel exhaled. He wanted to throw his arms around her or yell at her. He couldn't decide which.

"Thank God, you're both okay," he said. "Hannah, what were you doing here?"

"I wasn't investigating, Daniel. Samantha and I were going out for a pre-holiday drink. I was just waiting for her to finish her meeting with Palmer's lawyer. Who knew it was Vargas?"

"Your amazing wife saved my life," Samantha said. "I owe her, big time."

"What did you do?" Daniel asked.

"He didn't know I was here," Hannah said. "I ran up behind him and hit him on the head with a bookend. Can you guys call the ER later and make sure I didn't do any permanent damage?"

"I'm hoping she did," Samantha said. "He said he was going to kill me. As far as I'm concerned, I'd rather have him brain-dead than me."

"That reminds me," Hannah said. "you'd better take this."

She reached into her pocket and handed Brenda her phone. "When Samantha left the door to her office open, I figured she wanted me to listen, so I started recording. If a jury has any doubts about Vargas's intentions, this should clear them up."

"You are awesome!" Brenda placed the phone in an evidence bag. "The evidence team should be here in a little while. I'm going to need to get statements from both of you. Daniel, why don't you take Hannah home and bring her into the station tomorrow morning?"

"I'll drive Hannah's car home. Can you take my car to the station?" Daniel asked Leila.

She nodded.

"I can come in tomorrow, as well. Just give me a time. Tonight, all I want to do is go home, pet my cat, and have a large single malt Scotch," Samantha said.

"Sorry about the drink," Hannah said.

"No worries. I'm planning to take both of you out for the most expensive dinner in town once the holiday madness is over."

Daniel guided Hannah out the door and to the elevator. Then he put his arms around her and held tight.

"You have no idea how terrified I was," he said.

"Probably not as terrified as I was," she said, nuzzling her nose into the space between his neck and shoulder. "Sweetie, could you do one little thing for me?"

"What's that?"

"Can we stop at the Verizon store on the way home? There's no way an obstetrician can be without a phone."

CHAPTER THIRTY-EIGHT

D ANIEL SEEMED LOST IN THOUGHT AS THEY DROVE TO the Verizon store. Hannah could tell he was processing and suspected he would get it off his chest once they were home. She didn't want to talk now either. She was still shaking. It felt like a flock of pigeons was flying around inside her stomach. What if she'd caused a fatal brain injury with that bookend?

Daniel waited for her in the car while she went inside, purchased the most recent iPhone, and had her cloud backup transferred to it. There were no new texts or emails. Thankfully, she wasn't on call this weekend.

Zoe was waiting at the front door when they pulled into the driveway. "Mommy, why are you so late? Emilia and I baked cookies."

Hannah bent down and hugged Zoe, smelling the scent of floral shampoo in her silky hair. No matter how awful her day was, Zoe always made her feel better, although friends had warned her not to count on that once her daughter became a teenager.

"Cookies are just what I need," Hannah said. "I had to get a new phone. Mine died."

"Yours is always interrupting us," Zoe said. "It would be nice if it stayed dead. Do you want oatmeal or chocolate chip?"

"Definitely oatmeal," Daniel said, following the two of them into the kitchen.

Hannah and Daniel didn't talk until after Emilia left with her Christmas bonus and gifts, they had all eaten a late dinner, and Zoe had gone to bed. Wordlessly, the two of them followed her upstairs and into their bedroom.

"Okay, tell me what's on your mind. Are you angry at me?" Hannah asked.

"I asked you to lock yourself in an office and stay safe. Why the hell didn't you listen?"

"I had a choice," Hannah said. "I could hide like a frightened rabbit and let him kill Samantha, or I could do something. I would never have forgiven myself if I did nothing and she died."

"Did you think for one moment about me and Zoe, how we would have felt if you were killed too?"

"Daniel, I didn't have time to analyze the situation. I just acted. I saved Samantha's life. Why did you insist I take self-defense lessons if you never expected me to make use of them?"

Hannah started to undress, throwing her clothes on the chair and pacing the room.

"I wasn't looking for trouble. I was just meeting a friend for a drink. I know he's a killer, but I'm not. I'm still shaking and frightened that I may have ended his life. Just because he was alive when they put him in the ambulance doesn't mean I didn't cause a fatal brain bleed. I need empathy from you. What I don't need is for you to treat me like a disobedient child."

Daniel took a breath and reached for her. "I'm sorry. You have no idea how petrified I was when I found out Vargas was there. I was driving like a maniac trying to get to you. I can't imagine losing you." He drew her close and hugged her tightly.

"That's not going to happen. If anything, the odds are much higher that I could lose *you*. You deal with the worst scum on earth, every single day. You put yourself in danger to solve cases. But if I allowed myself to feel frightened every day you left here to go to work, I wouldn't be able to function."

"How do you deal with those fears?" Daniel asked.

"I realize neither of us can control every random event, but I remind myself that you are smart, resourceful and careful. I know you don't take any unnecessary risks and that you know how to do your job. I trust you to take care of yourself. I need you to trust my judgment as much as I trust yours."

"Point taken," Daniel said.

"By the way, do I need a lawyer when I go to make my statement?" Hannah asked.

"Having an attorney is always a good idea. Why don't you call Samantha in the morning for a referral?"

Hannah put a nightgown on and pulled down the duvet. "Okay, I will. Right now, all I want is a sleeping pill and oblivion."

CHAPTER THIRTY-NINE

Saturday, December 24th, 2016

As soon as Daniel awakened, he headed for the kitchen, careful not to disturb Hannah, who was still deeply asleep. He started a pot of coffee and phoned Brenda. "I hope I didn't wake you."

"Of course not. I'm always bright-eyed and bushy-tailed at 7:00 a.m. on a Saturday when I'm supposed to be off work."

"I'm sorry. Hannah's been so upset about the possibility that she might have killed Vargas or caused some permanent brain injury. She's not going to be able to think straight with this hanging over her. Do you know his status?"

"Tell her to relax. I spoke to his doctor last night. No skull fracture, no brain bleed, just a concussion. He's conscious and cuffed to the bed with a full-time police guard. As soon as he's discharged, we're transferring him to a cell in the station for questioning."

"That's a relief. Did you see him?"

"Read him his rights and allowed him a phone call. He

tried to reach Palmer, but wound up having to leave a message with Palmer's staff. Vargas may have a lawyer before we get to interrogate him. By the way, neither of us is permitted to question him. Conflict of interest due to our relationship with Hannah. The chief wants to play this by the book."

"You think Vargas will turn on Palmer to get a plea deal?"

"Hard to say. The prosecutor was impressed with Hannah's phone recording, by the way. You have one amazing wife."

"Tell me something I don't know. Speaking of Hannah, can her statement wait until Monday? I think she needs a little downtime. It's been a horrific experience her. For both of us, really."

"I'm sure Monday will be fine," Brenda said.

"Thanks," Daniel said. "And Merry Christmas.

Hannah rolled over at the sound of her new phone. Squinting at the light, she noted the time, 8:15 a.m., and the caller.

"Good morning, Samantha."

"Did I wake you?" Samantha asked.

"I was lying in bed, considering opening my eyes. How are you doing? Yesterday was hideous."

"Tell me about it. I didn't get much sleep, even with a considerable dose of Scotch."

"I didn't sleep well either. I guess we'll find out today if Vargas lived or if I killed him. Daniel told me I should ask you to recommend an attorney before they question me at LAPD."

"I'll be happy to find you an attorney, but you are a heroine regardless of whether Vargas is dead or alive to face trial. Not only did you knock Vargas on his ass, you had the presence of mind to record him saying he was planning to kill me. I've been wanting to call and thank you for saving my life. If you hadn't knocked the bastard out, I'd be dead and buried by now."

"You're welcome." Hannah sat up in bed, swinging her feet over the edge and slipping them into a pair of clogs. "But we're not done yet. I'm positive Palmer is the person behind Nicole's death. If Vargas dies, we'll never be able to prove Palmer's guilt."

"We need to figure out our next steps," Samantha said.

"Why don't you come over to our house around eleven today? I'll make brunch and we can brainstorm. Zoe has a play date later this morning, so Daniel and I are free."

After being sated with blueberry pancakes and strong coffee, Hannah led Samantha and Daniel into the den, where they spread out on the comfortable chairs and Samantha opened her briefcase.

"So, now what happens?" Hannah asked. "Clearly Palmer wasn't interested in negotiating a settlement with you. He preferred to see you dead, just like Nicole."

"The fact that Palmer sent Vargas to eliminate me gives us valuable information," Samantha said. "If Palmer had just drugged Nicole so that Fuchs could rape her, he would know for certain he wasn't the father of her child. Palmer could have demanded a paternity test to make the lawsuit go away. But he didn't."

"Therefore," Daniel said, "Palmer raped her too and

didn't know which of them had fathered her child. He couldn't take the risk of having a scandal just as he was about to become the nominee for Energy Secretary. Palmer must have tracked Nicole to Los Angeles and thought he could solve his problem by killing her and her unborn baby. When his initial murder for hire attempt failed, he sent Vargas to finish the job."

"Unless Palmer did it to protect Fuchs, or under orders from Fuchs," Hannah said. "Which raises the question of whether we can find any evidence for that. We know that Fuchs is Jeremy's biological father, but I sent out the genetic study under a fake name. The results won't be admissible in court."

"Fuchs raises the stakes to a whole new level, and I don't recommend even trying to get to him," Samantha said. "My priority, as the trustee for Nicole, is to protect Jeremy. I've done the best I can to place him safely and untraceably with a good family, but Fuchs has resources that could find him. If we go for Fuchs, we put Jeremy in danger."

"So, do you have a plan?" Daniel asked.

"I plan to file the lawsuit against Palmer first thing Monday morning and tip off the media. That should throw a wrench into his nomination and perhaps encourage Vargas to give up his boss."

"Does that really provide justice for Nicole?" Hannah said. "What happened to her breaks my heart. She was raped by both our president-elect and his right hand man, left a quadriplegic after the first attempt to kill her failed, and then murdered while she was lying helpless in a hospital bed, all to cover up their sick crimes. Even if we can pin it on Palmer, why should Fuchs get away with what he did? Besides, even if Palmer acted on his own with the murder, and Fuchs knew nothing about it, rape is still a felony. Having a rapist as the president of this country is unacceptable."

"We all feel the same way, Hannah," Daniel said. "But you need to ask yourself, what would Nicole want us to do? Samantha has done everything she can to give Jeremy a good home and protect him. Do you think Nicole would want to jeopardize her son's life by getting Fuchs involved? "

Hannah sighed. "No, obviously not. If Fuchs is a rapist, maybe some other woman will come out of the woodwork to accuse him. But the fact that he's going to get away with what he did to Nicole still eats at me."

"The three of us are the only ones who know this," Samantha said. "And if it gets out, we are all in danger. And Jeremy, and possibly even his adoptive family, will also be in danger."

"I know," Hannah said. "I hate what happened, but you can trust our discretion."

CHAPTER FORTY

Wednesday December 28th, 2016

D ANIEL AND BRENDA SAT AT THEIR ADJOINING DESKS, glued to their computers, which showed the video feed from the camera in the interrogation room. Vargas sat at the table, hands cuffed, his face unshaven, and his head wrapped with a white bandage. Leila entered the room, tall and elegant in a camel pantsuit, carrying a leather briefcase. She sat down, took out a file folder, and turned on the recording equipment.

"Mr. Vargas, I hope you're feeling better. I'm Detective Abebe. I know you were read your rights at the hospital and given a phone call, but I'm going to repeat them for the recording. I see you're alone. Have you waived your right to an attorney?"

"I don't need a fucking attorney. I haven't done anything."

"For the record, if you don't have a lawyer, we can call a public defender."

"Don't bother," Vargas said.

Daniel winced. "No need for her to offer again. She knows we're better off without one."

"She's covering her ass," Brenda said. "No one can say Vargas wasn't treated by the book."

Leila repeated Vargas' rights. "Do you understand what I've said to you, Mr. Vargas?"

"Just get this over with." He leaned back, looking bored and angry.

"For the record, what is your full name and what is your job?"

"Hector Vargas. I work for Kenneth Palmer. Perhaps you know the name. He's been nominated to be Energy Secretary for the Fuchs administration."

"What do you do for Mr. Palmer?"

"Whatever he needs. I arrange his schedule, meet with people he's too busy to see, recruit and screen high-level employees for his company, make sure his coffee is hot and black—as I said, whatever he needs."

"Did you fly to Orange County with him on Friday, December 24th in his private jet?"

"Yeah. He was attending a dinner and rally for the president-elect."

"Where did you go after your flight landed on Friday?"

"I drove to the office of Samantha Copeland in Los Angeles."

"And why was that?"

"She was threatening to sue Mr. Palmer for totally bogus reasons. He wanted me to negotiate an end to her efforts. He's too busy to spend time in court rebuking false charges."

"What charges were those?"

"That's confidential. The lawsuit hasn't been filed so its contents aren't public."

"I see," Leila said. "Who is Michael Rodriguez?"

"He's an attorney. Does some work for our company."

"You introduced yourself to Ms. Copeland using his name. Why was that?"

"She was expecting an attorney. I wasn't sure she'd negotiate with me, so I used his name. Is that a crime?"

Leila didn't answer. "Did you negotiate with Ms. Copeland?"

"Yeah. She gave me a number she was willing to settle for and said her client would sign an NDA. I called my boss and he told me to bring her to the hotel to sign the documents."

"Did Ms. Copeland agree to meet with your boss at the hotel?"

"Yes."

"Then why did you pull a gun on her to get her to go with you?"

"I didn't pull a gun on her. That's a lie. We were walking to the elevator and someone came up behind me and hit me on the head. I blacked out. When I find out who hit me, I'm filing charges."

"Can you explain then how a loaded gun, with your fingerprints on it, wound up in the waiting room of Ms. Copeland's office?"

"Someone must have framed me when I was unconscious."

Leila shook her head. "We have two credible witnesses who say otherwise."

"It's their word against mine. Why would I pull a gun?"

"Perhaps because Ms. Copeland didn't want to go with you in your car, and you wanted the opportunity to make sure she, and her lawsuit, disappeared for good."

"That's ridiculous. Why would I want to do that? I'm just the messenger."

"Exactly my question, Mr. Vargas. Unfortunately for you, we have a recording of you informing Ms. Copeland that you were planning to kill her. You're being charged with kidnapping and attempted murder. But the person with the motive here is your boss. Did he tell you to kill her? Were you just following orders? If you're honest with us, the prosecutor might be willing to cut you a deal."

Vargas was silent. Leila waited him out. Daniel chewed on his lower lip, wondering if he'd take the bait.

Leila broke the long silence. "Perhaps you didn't see the article on the front page of the Los Angeles Times."

She placed the paper on the table and passed it to Vargas.

Energy Secretary Nominee Sued for Rape and Paternity

Kenneth Palmer, recently nominated for Energy Secretary by President-Elect Fuchs was sued in civil court for rape and paternity by the estate of Ms. Nicole Adler. Ms. Adler, the recent victim of a hit and run which rendered her a quadriplegic, died from her injuries at Memorial Hospital. Mr. Palmer's attorney, Michael Rodriguez, denied the charges. President-Elect Fuchs' office had no comment.

"The civil lawsuit against your boss has been filed and the media is all over it. He's going to be tried for rape, and his nomination is in jeopardy. Still want to take the blame for him?"

Finally, Vargas spoke. "I think maybe it's time for me to get a lawyer."

CHAPTER FORTY-ONE

Thursday January 5th, 2017

WHEN DANIEL AND LEILA LEFT THE OFFICE OF THE prosecutor assigned to the Vargas case, they were both smiling.

"Well done," Daniel said. "You did an excellent job presenting all our evidence to the DA."

"Thanks. I hope he got how complicated this case is."

"Oh I think he got it, and he's willing to play ball and talk to the Feds. If we can use Vargas to nail Palmer, it'll be a big win for the Justice Department. Does Vargas have an attorney yet?"

"Yeah. When it became clear to him that his boss wasn't going to ride to his rescue with a high-profile defense lawyer, he agreed to meet with someone from the public defender's office. I'll interview him again tomorrow and see if that's changed his stance."

Daniel smiled. "I'm looking forward to watching you."

CHAPTER FORTY-TWO

Friday January 6th, 2017

THE PUBLIC DEFENDER WAS A MIDDLE-AGED CHINESE woman with short gray hair, wearing a navy blue pantsuit, and carrying a leather document case. Daniel sat at his desk, watching as she was escorted down the hall to the room where Vargas was seated. Leila gave them a few minutes to talk privately and then entered the room.

She turned on the sound and cameras, so that Daniel could follow the interview. "I'm Detective Abebe. Mr. Vargas and I have met before and I have read him his rights. This meeting will be recorded."

"I'm Mei Zhou from the Public Defender's Office."

Leila nodded and sat down. "Today is January 6th, 2017. Detective Leila Abebe interviewing Hector Vargas. His lawyer, Ms. Zhou, is present."

"Mr. Vargas, I will come directly to the point of this meeting. Yesterday, I met with the DA initially assigned to your case. You are being charged with attempted kidnapping, attempted murder, and first-degree murder."

"What the hell?!" Vargas said. "I didn't murder anyone."

"We beg to differ. We have security camera footage from the rehabilitation floor and the garage at Memorial Hospital showing you, disguised as a janitor, entering the room of a patient named Nicole Adler. Shortly afterward, she was found dead in her bed. Autopsy and forensic data demonstrated she was smothered to death with a pillow. We have additional evidence linking you to the hit and run that left her a quadriplegic."

"Don't say anything," Ms. Zhou said. "This was not the information I was given when I was assigned to Mr. Vargas. Who is this Nicole Adler?"

"You may have read that Mr. Vargas's boss, Kenneth Palmer, is being sued in civil court by the estate of a woman who accused him of rape and of being the father of her child. It made the front page of the Times recently. I will make sure that your office receives all the relevant evidence to review next week."

"Are you suggesting that my client murdered her on orders from his boss?"

"I'm not suggesting anything," Leila said. "Because your client lives in Texas, and traveled to California to commit these crimes, his case falls under federal jurisdiction. In California, there is no death penalty. But in Federal court, the maximum penalty for first-degree murder is death. If your client wishes to cooperate, the DA is willing to discuss the possibility of a reduced sentence with the Justice Department."

"My client will not make any decisions until I have had a chance to review all the material and discuss it with him in detail. I'll be in touch once he and I decide how he wishes to proceed. This interview is over," Zhou said.

"I look forward to hearing from you," Leila said, as she shut off the recorder. "Don't take too long."

CHAPTER FORTY-THREE

Friday January 20th, 2017

"W HAT ARE YOU WATCHING?" HANNAH ENTERED THE kitchen, dressed in scrubs, and headed in the direction of the coffee machine.

Daniel was at the table, glued to a video on his laptop. "Just the news. It's mostly the lead-up to the inauguration in an hour."

"Seriously? Do you want to watch Fuchs take the oath and make a speech? Just looking at his smug face nauseates me. Not to mention that he'll never pay for what he did to Nicole."

"I find that as frustrating as you do, but we'll have to settle for Palmer getting arrested and tried for murder."

"Do you know something I don't?" Hannah asked, as she added sugar and cream to her coffee.

"I know the Feds are negotiating a plea deal with Vargas's attorney. He's going to testify that Palmer instructed him to kill Nicole and paid him a bonus once it was done. The Feds are following the money trail to verify his statements. Once they have the evidence locked down, they'll arrest Palmer. This is confidential, by the way."

Hannah put two slices of sourdough bread in the toaster and sat down. "My lips are sealed. I'll be happy to read about the arrest in the L.A. Times or see it all over cable news."

The toast popped up and Hannah rose to get a plate and some butter from the refrigerator. She added butter and jam to her toast and slid the plate onto the table. Walking behind Daniel, she put her arms around him and kissed his cheek. Then she closed the cover on his computer.

"Let me cheer you up. Do you happen to remember what happened on election night?"

"How could I forget? Thinking about it is not cheering me up."

"Clearly," Hannah said, "you forgot the hot sex we had, to make ourselves feel better."

She pushed the breakfast table away and settled herself on his lap.

"That, I didn't forget."

"It turns out I wasn't thinking straight that night and I forgot I was ovulating. I've been waiting to tell you until I was sure I wasn't going to miscarry again. I'm pregnant. I'm twelve weeks along now. And the genetic studies are perfect."

Daniel's jaw dropped. "Really? What are we having? A perfect boy or a perfect girl?"

"We're having a surprise. We'll have to tell everyone to get us gender-neutral baby clothes."

"Can we tell Zoe?"

"Of course! And Josh. Then we'll tell our parents. I think my mother gave up on having another grandchild when I turned forty-two. They'll be thrilled. I'll probably become Memorial's poster doc for geriatric pregnancy."

Daniel drew her in for a long kiss. "Okay, old lady. It's time for your husband to start pampering you. Pickles and ice cream for dinner?"

"Just ice cream, thank you."

"Maybe 2017 won't be such a bad year after all."

EPILOGUE

August 5th, 2017

Hannah adjusted the angle of her hospital bed and lay back on the pillows, enjoying the scent and feel of the newborn baby nursing at her breast. The second delivery had been a piece of cake compared to the long labor she'd had with Zoe. The combination of an early epidural and a half-hour of pushing had produced a beautiful, curly-haired, brown-eyed baby and left her feeling energized and joyful.

She glanced over at the empty cot, where Daniel had spent an uncomfortable night. He'd taken a run downstairs to the hospital coffee shop. Hopefully, the three of them would be going home later this morning. Both she and Daniel were planning to take advantage of parental leave.

The door opened to a grinning Daniel holding a cardboard tray. "I got us large vanilla lattes and an assortment of coffee cakes," he said, placing the food on the side table.

"You are my hero. I should research how much caffeine

is secreted in breast milk. I wouldn't want to interfere with a nap."

Daniel reached for his child, who appeared to be done nursing, and swaddled the baby skillfully, placing the wrapped bundle in the Lucite bassinet at Hannah's bedside. Then he sat down next to her and handed over the coffee. "You will never guess what I heard in the coffee shop."

"Good news or bad news?"

"You decide. The television was on and our friend Kenneth Palmer was being interviewed on Fox News before his murder trial. I doubt either the interviewer or Palmer's legal team knew what he planned to say."

Hannah took a bite of her cinnamon coffee cake and followed it with a sip of latte. "Stop teasing. Let's hear it."

"He accused Fuchs of being a serial rapist. He said he'd been tasked with being his procurer. Fuchs would point out a woman he wanted, and Palmer's job was to entice her to a private room on some false pretext and drug her so that Fuchs could rape her without being recognized."

"Oh my God! Is he accusing Fuchs of having been Nicole's rapist and pleading that he was just following orders?"

"Something like that. Only he's claiming that Nicole wasn't the only one."

"Do you think other women will accuse him? Maybe Fuchs will be impeached."

"Fat chance," Daniel said. "His party controls the Senate. He could walk into a convention with an AK47, commit multiple murders, and the Senate wouldn't have the guts or the votes to convict him."

"Daniel, what if Fuchs tracks down Jeremy and tries to have him killed, so there can't be a paternity test?"

"I don't think he'd take the risk now. It's to his benefit if

Jeremy remains untraceable. A positive paternity test would cement his guilt."

"So, what now?"

Daniel shrugged. "Hard to say. There could be a congressional investigation, or the Justice Department could investigate."

"The attorney general is one of Fuchs' cronies. That's not going to happen."

"Whatever happens, maybe enough voters will see Fuchs for who he is, so he'll be a one-term President. In the meantime, you and I can focus on what is truly important. Our family."

Hannah drew him to her and kissed him gently. "I've never been a believer in the afterlife, but if there is one, and Nicole is up there watching the news, I hope she's satisfied."

ACKNOWLEDGMENTS

Many friends and colleagues contributed to this book and deserve my heartfelt thanks.

First, the usual suspects. My husband Uri has always been my biggest fan, first reader, and IT consultant. Linda Schreyer has edited all my books and I couldn't write one without her. My writing critique group, Darlene Basch, Laurie Collister, and Rick Draughon have given me invaluable feedback, chapter by chapter.

Kristin Bryant designed my wonderful cover, and Christiana Miller handled copy editing, formatting, uploading and marketing for me.

I've relied on several friends and colleagues for their medical expertise.

Dr. David Rudnick and Robin Grote have shared their knowledge of brain injury and amnesia. Dr. Sandra Rudnick and the late Dr. Wayne Dodge have educated me on what it is like both physically and psychologically to be quadriplegic, and Dr. Robert Klapper answered my questions on spinal surgery.

Finally, Jerry Bernstein made sure that my fictional attorney didn't make any legal errors, Ann Berlstein educated me on the legal aspects of adoption, and Lauren Bernstein was my guide to Instagram. I'm grateful to all of you.

ABOUT THE AUTHOR

PAULA BERNSTEIN is a New York native, who migrated to LA to attend graduate school in Chemistry. She acquired a PhD, an exceptionally nice husband, and the ability to synthesize creative meals from leftovers. Not long afterwards, she escaped her laboratory and attended medical school.

Like her series heroine, Hannah Kline, Paula spent her professional life practicing Obstetrics and Gynecology. When she developed an irresistible desire for an uninterrupted nights' sleep, she retired from her full time practice, and reinvented herself as a writer of medical mysteries.

Learn more about her at her website:
www.hannahklinemysteries.com

ALSO BY PAULA BERNSTEIN

The Hannah Kline Mysteries

Murder in the Family

Murder by Lethal Injection

Murder in a Private School

Murder in the Goldilocks Zone

Murder in Vitro

Murder on Her Honeymoon

Murder is a Nightmare

Murder is a Hate Crime

Murder is Paralyzing

Short Stories

Potpourri